# ENTROPY

### A Montague & Strong Detective Novel

## ORLANDO A. SANCHEZ

BITTEN PEACHES
PUBLISHING

## ABOUT THE STORY

**Every ending is a beginning, unless the ending is final.**

With the First Elder Rune divided between them, Monty and Simon must confront Keeper Gault and stop him from undoing reality and everyone in it.

There's just one obstacle.

The First Elder Rune is too strong for them, and not even an Archmage can help them now. As Gault strikes at those closest to them, he offers them one choice.

Surrender the rune...or everyone you know dies.

In order to harness the power of the rune, they must find a way to restore it without destroying themselves in the process. They have a plan and only one opportunity to make it work.

If they fail, Gault will capture the First Elder Rune, unleash entropy, and plunge the world into darkness.

*"The line between good and evil runs right through every human heart."*
*-Aleksandr Solzhenitsyn*

*"I am the spirit that negates.*
*And rightly so, for all that comes to be*
*Deserves to perish wretchedly;*
*'Twere better nothing would begin.*
*Thus everything that your terms, sin,*
*Destruction, evil represent—*
*That is my proper element."*
*— Johann Wolfgang von Goethe*

*"Every new beginning comes from some other beginning's end."*
*-Seneca*

## DEDICATION

*For Winter*

*We will always lovingly remember you as the most amazing dog on the planet. Wherever you are now, I hope you have a comfy bed, lots of snacks, and a huge field to run in until you get exhausted.*
*You were the best girl.*

*8323*

# ONE

Dex glared at me from across the courtyard.

I couldn't see his face clearly, but I felt his glare from where I stood.

"It's just us?" I asked, looking around. "Really?"

"I don't want you distracted," he said, "especially with your Director around. Your brain gets all addled, and I need you sharp for this."

"My brain isn't addled," I grumbled as he crossed the large courtyard. "I'd be sharper if we didn't do this before sunup."

"Do you even know what time it is?"

"Looks like the middle of the night to me," I said, pointing up at the sky. "What time is it?"

"Time for you to focus."

"I don't do *focus* before dawn or coffee," I muttered, mostly to myself. "This can qualify as cruel and unusual training."

"My apologies," he said as he turned to face me with a small bow. "I'm sure your enemies will consult with your calendar about the best time to kill you. If you're lucky, they may even bring you a mug of your favorite coffee before they blast you off the face of the earth—something like a going-away gift."

"Wow, was that necessary?" I said under my breath. "And they call *me* the smartass?"

"Because you are one," he replied. "One who's going to get himself killed one day."

"How did you even hear that?"

"You're not as quiet as you think," he said. "Ready?"

"No. Most of my brain is still asleep!" I called out in the dark, barely making him out. "What's so urgent we have to do this now?"

"Life and death rests in the moments between decisions, boy," he said. "Lately, your decisions have been about as arse-backwards as they can get. It's a miracle you're still alive."

"*My* decisions?" I said in protest. "Are you serious?"

"Does it *sound* like I'm joking?" he answered, and the air in the courtyard chilled. "*You* are the Aspis. *You* are the Marked One. *You* are the catalyst. If I were an enemy, who do *you* think I would target?"

I remained silent, because he was right.

But that didn't mean I had to like it.

"Aye, finally, it's starting to register," he continued. "You are the lynchpin. When Gault attacks—and he *will* attack—he will focus on *you*. Now: focus, boy."

"I am foc—"

I never saw the attack coming.

The first orb crashed into my chest, spinning me around. By the time I managed to get my bearings, the second orb punched me in the face, causing me to stumble backward... into a green teleportation circle.

The courtyard vanished around me in a green flash. When I realized where I was, I found myself thirty feet in the air looking down at the courtyard.

I unfortunately didn't possess the ability of flight, and so came crashing down onto the stone floor of the courtyard with a heavy dose of pain and agony: two of my constant companions.

I groaned in protest as I rolled over on my back. My curse flared with heat, healing my mostly superficial injuries—there was no healing my injured pride, though. I couldn't believe I had missed all the indicators of that attack. The fact that he had surprised me pissed me off. I should have, at the very least, sensed it.

"You should really watch your step," Dex called out. "I did tell you to focus."

"A little warning would've been nice," I said as I slowly got to my feet. "That was underhanded and dirty."

"Aye," he said. "No such thing as clean fighting where you're headed, boy. Nothing is fair. Your enemies will blast you when you're down and laugh while you die. They will give you no warning and attack when you least expect. This is the world you've entered now, and there is no going back."

"My morale is all bolstered now, thanks."

He laughed in the darkness.

I was under no illusion that I could beat Dex, but I wasn't going to let him bounce me around the courtyard. Yes, he was powerful, but I wasn't exactly powerless.

"Are you ready now, boy?"

I materialized Ebonsoul and let the darkflame cover my hand in response. Ebonsoul thrummed with power in my hand as the energy flowed through me. Black wisps of energy wafted up from the blade as the runes along its length fluctuated from red to gold to violet.

"Yes," I said, stepping into a defensive stance. "I'm ready."

"Aye," Dex said with a nod as he formed Nemain. "It seems you're taking this seriously now. Good. Let's see how ready you truly are."

"Just because I'm taking it seriously doesn't mean you

need to bring out your psychoaxe," I said, wary of his weapon. "You can be serious without that thing."

He paused and looked at Nemain, holding it up to his face. He turned to face me and grinned. I knew this was going to hurt.

"Where's the fun in that?" he said, still grinning. "I would be remiss if I didn't make you fear for your life. The more you bleed in training, the less you bleed in battle."

"I don't think that's how that saying goes."

I was taking it seriously, but I didn't know about taking it Nemain-level serious. He stared at me as he hefted his axe-mace in one hand, pain and suffering disguised as an ancient mage. His weapon filled the courtyard with a feeling of despair and death.

There's always a cost...always.

Ultimately, it's not the cost that matters, but whether one is willing to pay it. Right now, the cost I was looking at was steep.

He raced in again. I barely parried his axe as he rotated the weapon in his hand. That move was followed by a fist that would have broken several parts of me if I hadn't shifted my weight to one side, taking the blow on my arm instead of my face.

The fist sent me flying, causing me to land on my back, hard. The air rushed out of my body as I bounced a few times, coming to a stop just short of the courtyard wall.

"Looks like you're focused now, boy," Dex continued with a growl. "Even for an immortal, dying is a poor strategy. Is that the plan? You're going to defeat Gault by dying enough times to tire him out, and then you'll strike when he's exhausted?"

"I don't intend on dying being a part of *any* strategy I use," I said, spitting out blood. "Are you *trying* to kill me?"

Dex hefted Nemain again and gave me a grin.

"Not yet," he said. "We haven't gotten to *that* part of the training."

He dashed at me, taking one step and disappearing from sight.

I didn't know how old Dex was, exactly, and it didn't really matter—however old he was, he moved faster than anyone his age had any right to.

He reappeared as he closed the distance with a swing of his psychoweapon.

I barely had enough time to lift Ebonsoul to intercept the strike. As our weapons clashed, a mini-explosion of black, gold, and violet energy erupted around us.

"Not bad, boy," Dex said, grinning with our weapons locked. "Stopping Nemain is no easy feat."

"Glad...glad I could impress," I said, struggling to keep him from pushing me into the ground. "Feels...feels like you've been hitting the gym."

He laughed this time.

"The gym?" he said. "No, child. This is what is normally called 'old man strength.' Usually arrives around the time a man becomes a father and is reserved for those moments when the pups feel themselves grown and think they can best their elders."

"But you don't have kids...do you?"

"Didn't need to have them," he said, unleashing a fist into my stomach, which forced the air from my lungs with a whoosh. "Montagues and Treadwells are a large clan. Plenty of young ones to guide, teach, pound, and intimidate into the proper shape. Consider yourself part of the clan."

He swung his weapon around, lightly tapping me in the chest with the oversized mace head, sending me across the courtyard floor at speed. At this rate, I was going to learn every square inch of the courtyard by sliding across it.

I slammed up against the far courtyard wall with a crash,

cracking some of the stones behind me. I sat there, stunned for a few seconds as I tried to catch my breath with deep gasps.

A distant whistling triggered all the alarms in my brain, forcing me to roll to the side as Nemain buried itself in the stones where I had sat a moment earlier.

"What the hell?" I said, raising my voice. "I'd like to file a formal divorce from the Montague and Treadwell clan."

"Too late," he said, extending an arm. "Wasn't your choice to begin with."

"This training session is going to be short if you kill me in the process."

"What do you think Gault is going to do, boy?" he called back as Nemain dislodged itself from the wall and flew back to his outstretched arm. "You think he's going to ask for the First Elder Rune politely? He's going to rip it from you as painfully as possible, in the hope that its removal will destroy you."

"Well, shit," I said, rolling to my feet. "Evergreen said we couldn't give it back to him. How is Gault going to use it?"

"Gault isn't Evergreen, and Keeper Evergreen wasn't being entirely truthful."

"What?" I asked, shocked. "Are you saying he lied?"

"Lied? No. He bent the truth a bit, that's all," Dex said as he formed several green circles around the courtyard. "If he had told you the truth—that he could take back the First Elder Rune—would you have kept it?"

"Hell no," I said, keeping an eye on the placement of the circles. Nothing good could come of Dex creating teleportation circles. "I would've tried to give him his rune right back."

"Exactly," Dex said. "That's why he was less than honest with you."

"Less than honest?" I asked. "He lied. Call it what it is."

"He didn't lie, exactly," Dex answered, and I felt the

energy shift around the courtyard which meant it was time to move. "In that moment, he couldn't take the rune back, even if he wanted to. It would have destroyed his body."

"Sounds like convenient mage semantics," I said, picking up my pace, and moving to the side of the courtyard, near one of the walls. "He still wasn't totally honest."

"You needed the First Elder Rune," he said. "Korin would have finished you both if you didn't have it."

He formed a small, green circle in the air and tossed it at my legs. I jumped to the side and avoided it with room to spare. Once I landed, I started running.

"Can't hit me if I don't stand still," I said as I moved around the courtyard. "Now what?"

I regretted the words as soon as they escaped my lips.

"This," Dex said, forming three more green circles. "Watch your step."

"Ha," I said as I sliced through one of the circles with Ebonsoul, disintegrating it. I rolled from the second circle and ducked under the third, sliding forward unscathed. "Missed me."

"Nice acrobatics, boy," he said. "Shame it was just prolonging your death."

"What are you talking about?" I asked, slightly winded. "You missed me with all three."

"I know," he said. "But you missed the fourth."

He pointed up.

Above me, I saw a circle almost as wide as the area of the courtyard where I stood. It hovered several feet above my head. There was no way I was going to dodge it in time. I focused and let the darkflame envelop my arm as I thrust upward with Ebonsoul.

For half a second, I managed to slice through it—then it overwhelmed the darkflame with a blast of green energy and crashed down into me.

I found myself teleporting throughout the courtyard, from circle to circle. After the third teleport, I lost all sense of direction. By the fifth teleport, I wanted to throw up. By the tenth teleport, my vision was tunneling in, and it was all I could do to raise Ebonsoul as Dex waited for me at the next circle.

He didn't even swing Nemain.

He didn't need to.

By the time I saw him, I was so confused I barely knew my own name, much less be able to mount a solid defense against an attack. He held Nemain still in front of his body as I flew face first into the mace. He didn't even budge as we collided. Nemain flung me back, where I landed in a heap of agony.

I groaned as the pain rushed in, as if to remind me how bad a decision it was to request that Dex help me get ready for Gault.

"How long, Sprite?" Dex called out. "What was the time?"

"Two minutes and twenty seconds," Peanut said as she skipped over to where I lay. She crouched down, her face filling my field of vision. "Not bad, Mr. Simon. You lasted five seconds longer than yesterday. That's progress. Isn't that good, Uncle Dex?"

"Absolute rubbish is what it is," Dex said with a growl. "Once you go down, how long do you think my nephew will last? How long do you think your pup will last? You *have* to get this into your skull, boy. *You* are the lynchpin. You *cannot* go down."

"In battle, first to strike," Peanut said, keeping her voice low. "In defeat—"

"Last to fall," I finished. "Thanks, Peanut."

I slowly got to my feet, feeling every inch of my body protest with every breath, as Peanut stepped away.

"I still think you did good," she said under her breath.

"You can do a bunch of stuff in five seconds. Five seconds is a long time."

"Feels like a lifetime when I'm facing him," I said, matching her tone. "He hits hard."

"He only hits you this hard," she said with a sweet smile. "He must *really* like you."

"I wish he liked me less," I answered with a groan as I formed Ebonsoul again. "You better get clear in case he wants to show me how much more he likes me."

She moved off to the side, leaving the space between Dex and me clear.

"You can't be the last to fall," Dex said, his voice rough. "You can't fall...*period*."

"How exactly am I supposed to do that?" I called out to Dex, who was still across the courtyard. "I know for a fact you weren't even using all of your power."

"Aye," Dex said with a tight smile. "Then again, neither were you."

"I...I... You're right," I said, finally. "I wasn't."

"You think you're going to be able to hold back with Gault?" Dex asked, pointing at me as he approached. "This isn't just about you. You want the truth? I'll give you the truth. If you and my nephew just stand in Gault's way, then everyone you know—and everyone they know—will be dead. He will erase them from existence without a second thought."

"Stand in his way?" I said, my voice low. "You don't think we can beat him?"

"I do," Dex said, placing a hand on my shoulder. "The question is: Do you? Until you know you can, deep in your bones, all you'll be doing is standing in his way, but that won't stop him from destroying your life and the lives of those important to you. Is that what you want?"

"No," I said. "I want the threat of Gault removed from my life, from my world."

"Then you have to *know* you can beat him," he said. "I can't place that belief in you. You can't hold back when you face him. He won't."

"I know."

"So you'd better start getting serious," he said, giving me a glance before turning to Peanut. "Let's go, Sprite. Simon has a visitor. Give my regards to the Director."

Dex formed a large circle which Peanut stepped into. They both vanished from sight a second later as a figure approached the courtyard.

Michiko.

# TWO

She closed the distance with all the grace of a lioness on a hunt.

Her black combat armor seemed bulkier than before, and I noticed that she was holding a short blade similar to Ebonsoul. The length and color of the blade and the fact that it was covered in runic symbols were where all similarities to my weapon ended.

Unlike Ebonsoul, which glowed red, gold, and violet with hints of black accents, her blade glowed only a deep violet.

The other major difference was the smoke: black smoke covered her blade and wafted up from her weapon as she approached. The signature of her weapon was impressive.

I had felt something similar to it in the past.

"Is that a kamikira?" I asked, focusing on the blade, and wondering why she would have it drawn. "How? I thought those blades were rare enough to be nearly impossible to find."

She looked down at her blade.

"Yes, this is a kamikira, taken from a would-be assassin,"

she said, gazing at me. "I see Ebonsoul, like its wielder, has grown in strength."

"Do you intend on stabbing me with that thing?"

"That would depend on who and what you've become."

"I haven't *become* anything," I said, measuring my words carefully. "I'm who I've always been."

"Not true," she said. "You have changed."

"So have you," I said, absorbing Ebonsoul. "I hear the Dark Council is currently under new management. Well —*new*, old management."

"Are you calling me *old?*" she asked with a slight smile as she sheathed her weapon. "Are you certain you want to start our conversation with my *age?*"

"Better than drawn blades, but no, not in the least," I said, raising my hand in surrender. "I just meant—"

"I know what you meant," she said with a nod. "Yes, the Dark Council is currently under a blood rule, one which will be lifted soon if I can prevent a vampire civil war."

"Who wants a war?"

"I think the question is, who doesn't?" she said with a sigh, looking off to the side. "There are several groups within the vampire faction of the Dark Council who would prefer to see me relieved of my position. Permanently."

"It's not easy being Director," I said. "What about the mages and the werewolves?"

"Whoever thought joining those three groups into one faction was either mad or a genius," she said, focusing on me again. "It's difficult enough to keep vampires from attacking each other—but add in mages and werewolves, and the task becomes nearly insurmountable."

"You can do it," I said. "You've been doing it."

"At a great cost," she said. "Many of my kind have perished either through foolishness or intrigue. The losses have not been as acute in the other factions, though your future actions may change that."

"My future actions?" I asked, confused. "What do you mean?"

"When I first gave you Ebonsoul, it was simply a siphon—albeit a powerful one—but still *only* a siphon."

"It's a little more than that now."

"You have bonded to the blade, which I expected," she said. "What I did not expect was its transformation, or yours."

"I'm not following," I said, stepping back as she rested her hand on the sheath holding the kamikira. "What are you doing?"

She was still giving me stabby vibes, not that I expected her to run into my arms after not seeing each other since Japan. That would have really thrown me. The stabby vibes made me defensive, but to be fair, it was kind of her default setting.

"Do you know the purpose of kamikira blades?" she asked, "why they are so rare?"

"Aside from the obvious, you mean?" I asked, putting some more distance between us—not that it mattered. We were in an open courtyard with nowhere to hide or take cover. Not from an ancient vampire with a god-killing blade. Anywhere I moved, she could cover almost instantly. "I thought they were meant to kill gods."

"Immortals," she corrected. "Kamikiras were designed as a check and balance against gods—yes—but more importantly, they are the first and last line of defense against *dark* immortals."

She let the words hang in the air between us as she stared at me. This wasn't exactly what I pictured when I envisioned us meeting again.

"Dark immortals?"

"Yes," she said, her hand not moving from her blade sheath as she stared at me. "Dark immortals."

I had an idea why she was acting so twitchy. Verity had been spreading a rumor, an unfounded rumor—about my going dark.

I wondered what had given them *that* idea.

Somehow that rumor must have gotten back to Chi, who was skeptical of most things, but did not take chances.

"Is that why they're rare?" I asked, slowing my breathing. "Immortals felt threatened and started destroying them?"

"It is incredibly difficult to destroy kamikiras. The gods opted for hiding them in impossible locations, planes of destruction, null planes devoid of life...anywhere that wasn't this plane." She looked around. "Well, not *this* plane exactly."

"They feared them that much?"

"Not just the blades, but those who would wield them," she said. "The *kamikoroshi*—god slayers."

"Remove the weapons and kill the god slayers," I said. "Why would immortals go through so much trouble?"

"They didn't," she said. "Another group did—the *kage no fumetsu.*"

"The who?" I asked. "I've never heard of the *kaka fu manchu*. They sound dangerous."

She sighed and gave me a stare as she shook her head.

"*Kage no fumetsu,* and yes, they are dangerous and ruthless," she added. "They have been the enemies of the god slayers for centuries."

"What exactly are these *kage no fumetsu?*" I asked, making sure to get the name right this time. "I don't see what this has to do with me."

"It's loosely translated as 'dark immortals,'" she said. "They were the ones who hunted down the god slayers and hid the kamikiras. Now I hear rumors that *you* have become a dark immortal. Is this true?"

"How exactly would *that* happen? I'm not any kind of magic user."

"I didn't say dark *mage*," she said. "Dark immortals have other avenues to power. *You* are bonded to a hellhound. You are the most current Marked of Kali, and you currently bear a necrotic seraph blade which is also a siphon— one that is nearly a match for my kamikira. There is more," she said, staring at me. "There is dormant energy within you, energy that is beyond you. If anyone is a candidate for dark immortal, I would look at you first."

Fine. So Verity did have a reason to think I may have become a dark immortal, but as Monty liked to explain, correlation does not imply causation.

"We haven't seen each other in a while," I said by way of explanation. "Things have happened. Monty and I have faced some major threats. There have been changes."

"Have any of these changes been a step into darkness?"

"You can't believe everything you hear," I said, shaking my head. "Most of those rumors are vicious lies spread by Verity and those who belong to the Let's Kill Simon fan club."

"Why would such a *club* exist?"

"People feel threatened by things they can't control, especially mages."

She narrowed her eyes at me, glancing at my chest.

"I see. I also sense the essence of Izanami is waking in your blade. She could use a dark immortal more than a dying dark mage. If she possessed your body, an immortal body, you would become unstoppable. A true dark immortal."

"I'm not a *dark* anything," I answered quickly. "We should talk about this."

"That is why I'm here, aside from the fact that Dexter graciously invited me to his future school of battle magic," she said. "I wanted to see the truth for myself. I place no stock in rumors."

"Is that why you're here?" I asked. "You're looking for the truth? It's not that you missed me?"

She gave me a stare that nearly stopped me cold.

"Simon, we are bonded to each other," she answered. "Asking if I miss you is like asking if I miss my arms or legs. We are connected. I thought you understood this?"

"I do, it just seems that this bond we share is suffering from signal-jamming," I said. "All this talk about looking for the truth has me a bit confused. Wouldn't you already know if I had gone dark?"

"There are levels of darkness that only become apparent when it's too late," she said, looking off again. "By the time it becomes clear, there is usually only one solution."

"A major discussion?"

"Of sorts," she said, looking at me again. "I need to make sure."

"Ask away," I said. "I'll answer any question about my supposed turn to darkness."

"Words alone will not suffice."

"I had a feeling you would say something like that."

"Yes. I am here to make sure I have not equipped a dark immortal with an unstoppable bloodthirsty siphon," she said, narrowing her eyes, "which is also a necrotic seraph. A *conversation* is needed."

That she knew about the changes in Ebonsoul didn't surprise me. What surprised me was that she wanted to have a conversation about it—a real *conversation*.

That usually meant blood and pain.

"It's me," I said, outstretching my arms. "You know me. When have I gone dark? Never, that's when. We don't need to have a *conversation*."

"We do," she said. "Ebonsoul, though bonded to you, is *my* responsibility. *I* gave it to you. *I* allowed you bond to it, knowing the potential danger."

"Wait a minute, isn't Grey a dark mage?" I asked. "Aren't you worried about him taking over the world with his blade?"

"No," she said. "The Night Warden was not always a dark mage, and while no one is above corruption when exposed to power, he is much older than you. He has navigated the temptation of power many times over the centuries. His darkness was brought about in an attempt to save another, not in the desire for more power. You are different."

"I don't want more power," I said, anger lacing my voice at the implied accusation. "Are you saying that I'm becoming power hungry?"

"You are not listening," she said. "Grey is alive because of his bond with Darkspirit, his blade. That bond is the only thing keeping him alive. It is not the same with you and Ebonsoul. If Izanami awakens in your blade, she will have access to your life force. You are bonded to the blade, and so if she usurps your control and takes over your body, the danger she poses would be unfathomable."

"She won't."

"You will have to forgive me for not taking you at your word," she said. "If you have gone dark, I need to sever that bond...permanently."

"No severing of any kind is needed."

"We shall see," she said. "You managed to halt Dexter's weapon, Nemain. That was unexpected."

"By both of us, I think," I answered. "Even though I know Dex was holding back."

"So were you. Why?" she asked the question I had been wondering about ever since Dex left the courtyard. "Were you hesitant to reveal your dark nature to Dexter? Afraid of the consequences if he saw you as a dark immortal?"

"No—I mean, there is no dark nature *to* reveal," I said. "Where is this coming from? We haven't really spoken since

Japan, and now you want to face me in battle? What kind of catching up is this?"

"You do not truly know someone until you fight them," she said. "The promise of death strips away the lies we create, and destroys facades, revealing our true selves. I need to know who you *are* now."

"I don't *want* to fight you," I said. "What happened?"

"I was betrayed by several people who were close to me— people I respected, people I considered my family," she said, her voice filled with anger and sadness. "Then in the midst of the chaos of the blood rule, Verity informs me that you have gone dark: you *and* the mage. That it is *my* fault for providing you with a cursed blade, and letting you bond with it. That *I* am now responsible for your actions."

"And you believed them?"

"I will not be betrayed again."

"I didn't betray you, or *anyone* for that matter."

"Then what I later learned was a stormblood cast, was unleashed in the Wordweaver compound, a cast that resulted in many dead Verity agents," she said. "A cast you and the mage unleashed against agents that were merely doing their job."

"A job that included killing me and Monty, because they felt we posed a threat."

"Did you?"

"No, we didn't."

"Did you unleash the stormblood?"

"Yes, but we weren't a threat," I said, knowing how it sounded. "There were extenuating circumstances. You really had to be there. We weren't the threat. We were *responding* to a threat."

"You responded to this threat by nearly destroying the Cloisters and New Jersey?" she asked. "How were you planning on convincing them of your harmlessness? By obliterating the rest of the city?"

"I never said I was *harmless,*" I said, letting the frustration creep into my voice. "But we are *not* a threat to the city, and *never* have been."

"The DAMNED would say otherwise," she said. "Should I send you Ursula's reports on your activities? You, your hellhound, and the mage have posed the greatest threat to the city for some time now."

"We protect the city, not threaten it."

"You protect it from threats?" she asked. "Is that what you are asserting?"

"Yes," I shot back. "We protect the city."

"From external threats?"

"Of course from external threats!"

"Who protects it from the internal threat you three pose?"

"What? I don't follow."

"Let me rephrase the question."

"Sure, why don't you make it real simple for me?"

"A Keeper has declared war on the city," she said, keeping her voice low and menacing. "A war on *my* city, unless a specific First Elder Rune is returned to him. Are you familiar with this turn of events?"

"I'm not aware of this declaration of war, no."

"Do you know who this Keeper is?"

"Yes, his name is Gault," I said, "one of the five Keepers of the Arcane runes."

"Now he wants to destroy the city—my home—because of this rune. The rune *you and the mage* possess, correct?"

"It's my home too."

"Which is precisely why he is threatening it," she said, drawing her blade. "Because of you, because of you, and the mage, and this rune you both have."

"Yes," I said, forming Ebonsoul as she nodded. There was only one way to set her mind at ease. We were going to have to have a *true conversation*. "And we're not giving it back. He's going to have to kill us first."

"I had a feeling that would be your response," she said. "Let me see if I can surmise the rest. This Keeper poses an existential threat to the city, or the world, or reality as we know it, or possibly all three—and only you, your creature, and the mage can deter him from his path of destruction."

"I don't know if we *can* stop him," I said, sliding into a defensive stance. "What I *do* know is that giving him that rune would kill us all."

"It's always the end of the world with you three," she said, sliding into a defensive stance of her own. "Did you ever stop to think that maybe the population of the city didn't want or *need* your saving?"

"What are you saying?"

"No one appointed you three the saviors of the city," she said. "Why do you act like it's your responsibility?"

"Because it is," I said. "If I have the power to do something, and do nothing, I'm just as responsible. I'm not going to stand by and just watch."

"Even if your actions get people killed?"

"What's the alternative? Do nothing and let even more people die?" I shot back. "I'm not going to let people die for nothing. Not on my watch."

"No, you would rather have them die for your misguided sense of justice and honor," she said. "They are just expendable victims to you, a disposable means to your ends of 'saving' the city. Is that the case?"

"You're wrong," I said as anger replaced the hurt I felt earlier. "Everything you've been told is a lie."

"Your way is the *only* true way," she said. "Spoken like a

true dark immortal. Only *you* can save those who need saving. Only *you* have the ability. Only *you* have the power."

"You are so wrong," I said, getting my anger under control. "Why would you believe the lies? They lied to you. It's all lies."

"I see," she said as black smoke wafted up from her blade. "Why didn't you attack Dexter fully?"

"Because I didn't want to hurt him."

As soon as I the words escaped my lips, I knew it was the wrong answer.

"Hurt him?" she asked, incredulous. "You were worried about hurting the most powerful mage I have ever encountered?"

"Yes."

She set her jaw and stared at me.

"The only way you could even conceivably imagine that you could hurt Dexter Montague is if you have an inordinate amount of dark power to tap into. Is that the case?"

"Does it matter if I say no?"

"No, it doesn't."

She lunged forward and attacked.

# THREE

She was fast.

Faster than I remembered.

One moment she was several feet away, the next she was in my face, attempting to bury a blade in my abdomen.

I parried her thrust and pushed her back.

She stepped back and stared at me.

A strange look was on her face; it was a mix of disbelief and admiration.

"The Simon I knew wouldn't have been able to parry my attack," she said. "He wasn't fast enough."

"I've changed," I said. "That doesn't mean I've gone dark."

"Prove it," she said, stepping forward with another thrust.

I jumped back just out of range as she closed again. She slashed at my midsection, forcing me to dodge as she buried a kick into my side, sending me sprawling across the stone floor.

I rolled to the side as she sped forward and buried her blade into the ground where I had been moments earlier.

I kicked out and connected with her leg.

It would've been easier to kick an I-beam. Softer, too. The shock of the impact reverberated through my body as I quickly changed strategies to one of survival.

She whirled on my location and backhanded me to the other side of the courtyard. I landed hard and slid for several feet.

I barely had time to react, rolling to the side as she crashed into the stone floor, leading with a fist where my head had been.

"Don't do this," I said, backing up. "There's no need for this."

"You can't run from me forever," she said. "Accept your fate and face me. Show me who you truly are, Marked of Kali. Unleash your darkness and face me true, as the dark immortal that you are."

"I am not a dark immortal."

"Embrace what you are," she said. "You may lie to everyone else, but don't lie to yourself."

Something snapped and the burning rage that threatened to cloud my reason switched to a cold, seething fury. I focused and let the darkflame flow within me. Black flames covered Ebonsoul and crept up my arm as I leaned against the wall, and slowly got to my feet.

"Is this what you wanted to see?" I asked, letting the flames engulf Ebonsoul. "If you think this power makes me dark, then you never knew who I was, not really."

"You *have* gone dark," she said, her voice grim and tinged with sadness. "I'm sorry, Simon. I cannot allow your bond with Ebonsoul to continue. I must sever it."

"You're welcome to come try."

She moved even faster this time, but it wasn't fast enough. The darkflame had heightened my reflexes and reaction times. She slashed at my wrist, trying to disarm me.

I absorbed Ebonsoul and produced it a moment later in my other hand. She had overreached in her attack, giving me an opening. I swung my hand down, crashing it into her wrist and forcing her to drop her blade.

It fell to the floor and I kicked it away.

She backed up and slid into a defensive stance.

Even unarmed, she was beyond dangerous, but I had Ebonsoul and the darkflame. We weren't evenly matched, but I was closer than I had ever been in the past.

All I needed was another opening.

She lunged forward, leading with a fist. I slipped the attack, moving to the side as she buried her fist in the wall behind me. She pulled out her arm, driving it sideways in a horizontal slash designed to remove my head as I ducked.

It was the opening I needed.

*This life is yours to take. Take it and grow in power.*

*I thought I told you to shut the hell up.*

I reversed Ebonsoul in my grip and drove it forward and up, stopping half an inch from her neck.

It would be a simple thing to remove her head from her shoulders.

"Do it," she hissed. "You know you want to. Kill me. I can see the desire in your eyes. Finish it. Unleash your true self. Let the darkness claim you."

What was she trying to do? Did she really want to die, or was this some elaborate test? In that moment, I let my senses expand—she was much stronger than she was letting on. Like Dex, she was holding back. Unlike Dex, she wanted to know if I had really gone dark.

Part of me was hurt that she needed to confirm it this way. I understood her motivation; I'd probably do the same thing if I were her. Still, on some level, it hurt that she felt the need to verify a rumor.

I reabsorbed Ebonsoul.

I stepped back and shook my head.

"Did I pass?" I asked. "Or do you want to test me again?"

She extended an arm, and her blade flew into her hand. She sheathed the kamikira and stared at me.

"I needed to make sure," she said. "I sensed Izanami, but you suppressed her with ease."

"You don't trust me."

"The allure of power has brought down and corrupted more than I can count," she said, looking away. "Your situation is...unique. You were not born into this life. Power—the promise of power—is enticing for even the strongest."

"So, basically, you don't trust me."

"If I didn't trust you, Ebonsoul would never have been in your possession," she said, still looking away. "I had to make sure your bonds were intact, that Izanami could find no purchase within you to spread her corruption."

I understood her concern.

"She tried to sever my bond with Peaches," I said. "That was her first and last mistake. No one and nothing is going to break that bond while I'm alive."

"She will try again," Chi said. "All she has is time. You must always be on guard. You must be vigilant, always."

"I know," I said. "I intend to have a conversation with Grey when I get a chance. Maybe he can offer me some advice."

"I don't think proximity to his blade would be such a wise choice at the moment," she said. "If you want some advice on dealing with Ebonsoul, I can only offer this: focus and strengthen the other aspects of your blade."

"I don't follow."

"It's not only a siphon now. You must study and develop the other aspects of the blade. Strengthen them in Ebonsoul and in yourself. It will diminish the power of Izanami's essence in the blade."

"It's a necrotic seraph—that means I either have to visit the dead or go deal with demons," I said. "Neither of those options sound like something I want to actively do."

"I didn't say it would be easy or desirable," she said. "You can't run from who you are. That blade is as much a part of you as one of your limbs. You and Ebonsoul are one, Marked of Kali."

"Oh, not dark immortal? Cursed for all time to live in the shadows of evil?"

She gave me a look, and a thin smile crossed her lips.

"You can be too much sometimes," she said. "But I would never think you a *dark* anything. For one, I think your creature would maim you, repeatedly, if you went dark. Not to mention your mage would make it his mission to end you if you truly decided to walk a path of evil. Choosing you for Ebonsoul was not happpenstance. You are not dark, despite being exposed to Izanami."

"I think I was saying that when you started."

"I know, but I had to see what influence, if any, she had on you," she said. "If she did manage to take over—"

"You would sever the bond."

"Yes," she said. "Ebonsoul is the check and balance to Darkspirit. I gave it to you because I felt you could deal with the essence of Izanami should the need arise, and stop Grey if he ever surrendered completely to her."

"I thought they were part of a set?" I asked. "How can I stop Grey if he has the other part of the set?"

"They *are* part of a set, but the blades depend more on the wielder than the essence contained within," she said. "Grey can control his blade, but if he ever loses that control—"

"I have to face him?"

"You have to *stop* him."

"You expect me to stop Grey, a dark mage older than Monty and considerably more powerful than most mages I know, besides Dex?"

"Yes, I do," she said without hesitation. "If he surrenders to Izanami, he presents an existential threat. I did not give him Darkspirit. My brother...Ken allowed emotion to cloud his judgment when he gave it to your mage."

"Who gave it to Hades for safekeeping."

"Who in turn used the blade for his own hidden purpose, by giving it to Grey along with his failed apprentice," she said. "Hades, I do *not* trust. He likes to operate from the shadows. He may, one day, try to influence Grey into surrendering to Izanami."

"I hope that day never comes," I said. "Grey may be a cranky old mage, but he's one of the good ones."

"I know. I hope it never comes to pass, but we must hope for the best—"

"And prepare for the worst," I finished. "Do you remember the last words you shared with me in Japan?"

She glanced at me and nodded.

"I do," she said. "*Koi no yokan.*"

"I looked it up," I said. "Do you still believe it?"

She stared at me directly now, slightly unnerving me with her penetrating gaze.

"Yes. It is why I tested you today," she said. "If you had been corrupted by Izanami, or truly gone dark, I would have had to end you."

"End me?" I asked. "I'm not exactly a pushover, you know. Even if you were holding back, I would've lasted at least ten seconds, maybe more."

"Do you think you can fight me on equal terms?"

"Equal terms? Probably not, but you have to admit—"

She vanished from sight.

And reappeared a second later behind me, gently placing the kamikira against the side of my neck.

"What would you like me to admit?"

"That the idea of leaving my head attached to my neck is a good one?"

# FOUR

"For once, we agree," she said, tapping the side of my neck with the flat of her blade. "You *have* grown in power, as has your mage, but you still have much to learn and so much more to grow. There are forces moving against you that you are ill-prepared for. We will do our best to make you ready."

"That sounds painful."

She removed the blade from my neck and faced me with a smile as she placed a hand against my cheek.

"It will be," she said. "As long as you understand the source, you will be able to bear any burden."

I nodded.

"Wait, you said '*we*'—what do you mean, *we*?"

"Has the basic understanding of English left you?" she asked, tapping my cheek in a slap reminiscent of Karma. "We, as in plural, more than one. Your attacks were full of openings, you didn't commit when you should have...and why exactly are you holding back?"

I was about to answer when she squeezed my face in a death grip.

"You must not apply half measures when you face this

Keeper," she continued. "Dex informs me we cannot help you face this adversary directly, but we can help you prepare."

She released the death grip and I rubbed my face.

"Dex knew you were going to test me?"

"Of course," she said. "Why do you think I'm here? I'm certain Roxanne is doing something similar with your mage even as we speak."

That thought brought a smile to my face.

"I thought you were here because Gault would target you," I said. "To make me suffer."

She answered with a smile that chilled my blood. The little voice in my brain screamed that the best place for me right now was as far away as possible from where she stood.

I stopped myself from taking a step back and clamped down on the oppressive fear surrounding me.

She nodded in approval.

"I am the Director of the Dark Council," she said. "More than that, I am the Reaping Wind. This Keeper will find that I am not such an easy target to eliminate."

The fear dissipated instantly as she wrapped her arm in mine in a rare display of affection as we crossed the court-yard. I looked up to see the lightening sky and my stomach clenched.

"The dawn," I said, suddenly worried. "Are you wearing Daystrider armor?"

"This is not *our* plane," she said, looking up into the sky. "That is not a true dawn. Didn't Dex tell you the days here are simulated? I think I will rather enjoy seeing a dawn again after so long, even if it's not real."

I nodded in relief.

"How soon do you have to get back to the Dark Council?"

"Soon," she said, her expression darkening. "The blood rule is still in effect. Until I recommend Ken as Director, and other clan heads I trust as Assistant Directors, my presence is a necessity."

"You're stepping down?"

"Yes. I can do more from the shadows than as a Director in the light," she said. "I will still be actively involved, but without the title."

"Or responsibilities?"

"The responsibilities will never cease, title or not," she said. "Ken did an admirable job while I was otherwise occupied, despite his complaints."

"Will he command the same respect you do?" I asked, concerned. "Somehow I don't get the same *I will rip you to shreds* vibe from him."

"Are you implying you fear me?"

I gave the question some serious thought. It wasn't too different from the question Badb Catha had asked me not too long ago.

*Do you fear Michiko?*

*What? No. Why would I fear her?*

*She's an ancient vampire, the leader of a large group of vampires, all highly trained to kill, and she is, after all, the Reaping Wind. That is no small matter. There are many who fear her, even within the Dark Council—especially within the Dark Council.*

I searched my feelings.

I knew how dangerous she was. I had seen her in action plenty of times and realized facing her as an enemy, a true enemy, would be a lethal situation—a situation one of us wasn't walking away from.

But I didn't fear her.

I feared her potential for absolute unwavering and nightmarish destruction, but I didn't fear the person she was. It's possible my feelings were biased, but somewhere deep, really deep, I knew that at her core she was a good person.

"No," I said, my voice full of conviction. "I don't fear you."

She turned at the sound of certainty in my voice.

"Some would call you a fool," she said. "They would tell you that having emotions and feelings for a creature like me could only end in your ruin."

"What would *you* call me?"

"I would hope that the person I chose to bestow Ebonsoul to would not depend on the opinions of others, not even mine, to form his conclusions."

I nodded.

"*Koi no yokan*," I said. "Nothing is changing that path."

"You realize that may take time—not years, but decades or centuries," she said quietly as the sky lightened in the simulated dawn. "Are you prepared to invest that much time?"

"Time happens to be one thing I do have," I said. "You know my answer."

"I do," she said, tightening her grip around my arm. "Your choice will be tested countless times in the coming years."

"I know," I said. "Is that also why you're stepping down from being Director? To step away from all the attention? Is that why you're installing Ken as Director?"

"Once the blood rule is rescinded, I know he will make an excellent Director," she said. "It suits him. And I'm not *installing* him—the remaining clan heads will have to agree."

"Right," I said with a shake of my head. "Would these be the same clan heads that will be aware of your presence in the shadows? Out there, waiting for them should they do something you feel would endanger Ken or the Dark Council?"

"You have a very devious mind, Simon Strong."

"Call them like I see them," I said. "You say you're not installing Ken; I say you're making the environment highly favorable to his being the next Director. I still don't see him being as scary as you, but I do think he can do the job."

"He won't need to be as fearsome as me," she said. "And as you said, those who would rise against him have either been eliminated or convinced that for the good of the Dark Council, it would be best if they cooperated with the new Director."

"It doesn't hurt that you're still out there in the shadows, in case they need a deeper, more convincing conversation," I said. "Something you can't do if you're the Director."

"True," she said. "The fear of the unknown is an effective deterrent."

"What are you going to do after that?" I asked. "After Ken and the clan heads take over in your place?"

"You mean, what are *we* going to do?"

Now I was really confused.

The simulated sun rose and she paused to gaze at it, lost in her thoughts. I always took it for granted, just being able to walk in the sun. For her, even something as simple as that could be lethal.

"What do you mean?"

"Another reason for my stepping down is to restore the safety of my city for my kind," she said. "That has changed."

"Changed? How?"

"There are still Blood Hunters in my city," she said, her voice laced with menace. "I am going to invite them to vacate my city."

"A purge will start a war," I said warily. "Valentina isn't going to like that. She's going to push back, and push back hard."

"If only it were that simple," she said. "The Blood Hunters Valentina leads are not the issue. They can be cowed and dispatched if need be. They are not the focus."

I didn't know what concerned me more: the fact that she shrugged off a war with the Blood Hunters, or that she felt they were easily intimidated and easy to dispatch.

"What or who is exactly the issue?" I asked. "You know if I go to war with the Blood Hunters, they're coming after me. We made a pact."

"Which will be null if you are attacked—according to your words and the pact you formed," she said. "Do you recall the blood oath you formed with Valentina?"

"Every day," I said, thinking back to the oath I formed with Valentina, the current leader of the Blood Hunters. "They've held up their end of the oath so far."

My conversation with Valentina's came back to me:

*This is a blood oath. If you break this pact, everything and everyone you love and hold dear, will be stripped from you and destroyed. This I promise.*

*I understand. I will make a promise of my own. If any blood hunter touches anyone under my protection, vampire or otherwise, I will make it my personal mission to erase your order from the face of the earth as long as I live.*

*We are in agreement. We will speak soon, Chosen of Kali.*

"As long as they don't touch anyone close to me or anyone under my protection, I can't take action against them, even if they are your sworn enemies," I continued. "I'm not trying to start a war with them. If I do that, every vampire and everyone close to me will be in instant danger."

"I'm aware of the conditions of the blood oath," she said. "I was there, after all. They did try to eliminate me with a final death."

"Then what are we talking about?" I asked. "Do I even want to know?"

"You don't have a choice," she said. "You made a blood pact that will have to be broken."

"Not by me, it won't," I said. "I'm not breaking the blood pact."

"I never said *you* would."

"I haven't attacked any Blood Hunters," I said. "What *are* you saying? Did Valentina—?"

"Estilete has resurfaced."

She let the words hang between us for a few moments before continuing.

"She has a following that the Blood Hunters cannot control, and her group has a target," she continued. "Would you like to know who it is?"

It was an easy guess.

The last time Esti and I crossed paths, I had forced her to learn how to fight with her off hand—by removing one of her arms. I was pretty sure she still held a grudge about that.

Valentina had refused to end her life, or to let me do so, claiming Esti was one of hers. It looked like that was one act of mercy that was coming back to bite everyone in the rear.

"Me?"

"As I said, you made a blood pact that will be broken."

"Estilete is going to break it, isn't she?"

She nodded.

"She will strike the moment you least expect, in a manner you cannot foresee," she said. "It is the Blood Hunter way."

"I'm not a vampire," I said. "I mean, fine, I did release a cast that took her arm, but I'm not her sworn enemy."

"It would seem there is some latitude in the inclusion of enemies for the Blood Hunters," she said. "It has been made known they are not fond of you, or our...situation."

"She brought that on herself," I said. "We fought, she cheated, and she lost. I understand revenge for the arm. I don't understand the rest of the hatred."

"You stopped her from killing *me*," she added. "Something she has eagerly desired for some time."

"So this is payback?"

"No," Chi said. "This goes beyond vengeance. She will want you to suffer. From my reports, she's even more deranged now and those who follow her are just as bad or worse."

"What is Valentina saying?" I asked. "She should be informed."

"Do you really believe Esti could resurface without Valentina's knowledge?" Chi asked. "Do you think she is unaware what one of *her* blood hunters does? The only real question is whether this has been officially or unofficially sanctioned."

"What if Valentina doesn't know?"

"Simon, if I know, I can guarantee you that Valentina knows."

"We should meet, then, before we start a war with them."

"I am open to discussing the terms of Esti's demise," she said. "The blood rule will be rescinded within days, and then I am stepping down and into the shadows."

"So you can hunt."

Her sudden retirement from being Director made more sense now. If she felt the vampires in the Dark Council were in danger, she would be more effective at handling any threat away from the Council than leading it.

By having Ken as Director, she still had access to Dark Council resources. For her, it was the best of both worlds. For Esti, this was going to be a nightmare of epic proportions—if she lived that long.

"So *we* can hunt," she said. "Rest assured, everyone you know is in danger. Everyone. You will have to honor the words of the blood oath."

"We speak to Valentina first," I said. "Then we decide if war is needed. I'd rather avoid turning the streets of the city into rivers of blood."

"As would I," she said. "A war benefits no one. Even one with the Blood Hunters would only serve to reduce our population. There would be unacceptable casualties on both sides."

"You think she's going to attack soon?"

"I don't know," Chi said. "But the best time to attack would be when you are dealing with another, more pressing threat, don't you think?"

"A threat like the Keeper and his Dark Arcanists."

She nodded.

"Survive your ordeal with this Keeper, and we will speak with Valentina before we deal with Estilete and her Blood Hunters," she said. "I have placed guards—surreptitiously of course—at the Moscow and the Randy Rump, as well as the NYTF Headquarters. She hasn't made a move yet, but she will."

"It's not like I have other things going on," I said. "I'm sure I'll be able to fit a group of deranged homicidal Blood Hunters into my calendar somewhere."

"They are no longer considered part of the Blood Hunters," she said. "According to my sources, they honor no cease-fire and every one of my kind is a target. Esti has broken completely from the Blood Hunters and has joined the Sanguinary Order."

"The what?"

"She has become a Blood Heretic," Chi said. "Think Blood Hunter, but fanatically driven to exterminate what they feel is a blasphemy against their beliefs."

"That blasphemy being vampires?"

"Correct," she said. "Throughout history, the Blood Heretics have been a more radical and dangerous faction of Blood Hunters, bordering on zealotry. I thought they had been wiped out, or at least sufficiently diminished in number as to be inconsequential. I was wrong."

"Groups like that have a habit of surviving," I said. "Is Valentina going to do something about these Heretics?"

"Do something?" she asked "What do you think the Blood Hunters would do?"

"They're not going to stop them?"

"Stop them?" she asked, shaking her head. "Simon, their purposes are aligned. The only difference is in execution. Blood Hunters follow a specific doctrine and have rules of engagement."

"Aren't the Heretics just ex-Hunters, like Esti?"

"No, the Heretics do not draw from Hunters to fill their ranks," she said. "Esti must have become extreme for them to accept her in their ranks."

"They have to have some kind of rules of engagement too," I said. "Even the most deranged enemy I've faced has some kind of rule of engagement."

"You have never faced Heretics. They have no such limitations. They only have one purpose: rid the world of my kind. There is no negotiation, no reasoning, no discussion of justice, or the idea of right and wrong. They relentlessly pursue one goal: the annihilation of my kind."

"How do you face an enemy like that?"

"Simple—you kill them, before they kill you," she said. "Everything else is pointless and a waste of time."

"If they have an Order, they have to have some kind of leadership," I said. "We could reach out to them and work something out."

She stared at me for a few seconds and then gave me a sad smile before shaking her head.

"There are times I forget how young you are," she said. "Reaching out to the leadership of the Order would be an exercise in futility."

"We could at least try. My diplomacy has gotten better."

"Your diplomacy?" she asked with a raised eyebrow as we headed into the main building. "Are you referring to the destruction before or after this diplomacy is employed?"

"Before," I said. "The destruction that happens after is usually Monty and Peaches, not me."

"You cannot reason with them, Simon," she said, her voice serious. "This is not a matter to be discussed at the moment. As you said, you have other concerns to attend to. I will do my best to weaken them before our confrontation."

"Will you reach out to Valentina?"

"As a courtesy, yes, to honor your blood oath," she said. "But I am certain she knows what Esti has done, what she has become, and what she is planning to do."

"Maybe Valentina can't stop her," I said. "Maybe this Order is too powerful."

"If that is truly the case, Valentina is in as much danger as you are," she said. "Esti will not hesitate to remove her if she feels Valentina has betrayed the Blood Hunters."

"Betrayed, as in making a blood oath with me?"

"Precisely," she said, letting go of my arm. "She would view a pact with you as a traitorous act, one deserving of death."

"Is there anyone else we can call for help? Don't you have something similar to this Sanguinary Order, but not psychotic?"

"Yes, it's called the Dark Council, but I will not lead them against the Order in a war of attrition," she said. "We will use...other methods to face this enemy."

I nodded.

She was right, and while I had never really faced an enemy like this, I had a feeling Keeper Gault was going to be close. We were headed further into the main building when I heard the explosion.

# FIVE

We ran over to one of the rooms at the far end of the floor.

Green smoke billowed out into the hallway, followed by a smoky Dex who stepped out to intercept us.

"Stay back," he said, holding up a hand, "I need to get this under control." He turned to Chi. "Director, there's a message for you in the office. Mo is holding it for you. Simon, wait there—I may need your assistance, boy."

Chi gave me a short nod and headed off.

"What is that?" I asked, keeping my distance from the green smoke. "What's burning?"

Dex held up a finger and stepped back into the smoke. A few seconds later, I heard another rumble from the room, followed by a thunderclap. Dex flew out of the room and crashed into the opposite wall.

I took a step forward and he held out his hand again.

"Don't even think about it, boy," he said and gritted his teeth. "Give me a moment. Wait right there. Don't move."

I took a few steps back, just in case Dex lost control of whatever he was working on. More rumbles filled the hallway followed by another thunderclap. He stepped out of the room a few seconds later. His clothes were gently smoldering, green smoke wafting up from his body.

More green smoke billowed out after him, but the rumbles were gone.

"What was that?" I asked warily. "Are you summoning stormbloods in that lab?"

"One of my pet projects," he said. "Something I have Peanut working on."

"You're having Peanut mess around with stormbloods?" I asked, slightly shocked. "Is she strong enough to deal with a stormblood?"

"Not stormbloods," he said, looking from side to side. "Something else."

"Something else?"

He stared at me and slowly closed the door.

"Come with me," he said. "Now."

He had gone totally cloak-and-dagger on me. At every intersection, he would pause and look from side to side before proceeding. I was under the impression that the school grounds were mostly empty, but from his behavior, he was acting like he was avoiding someone.

"What is going on?" I asked. "Who are we avoiding? Are you trying to avoid the Morrigan?"

He shot me a look and held his finger to his lips.

"Talk later, walk now."

His voice didn't allow for any argument as I followed him down some stairs, to a darkened corridor, which led to another room. The door on this room was made of rune-covered Australian Buloke and radiated a signature of *Stay away or die a horrible and agonizing death*. I made sure to keep back from the door.

Dex placed his hand on the door, causing the red and gold runes to become subdued, dimming in their glow as he slowly opened the door.

"This way," he said, stepping into the room. "Follow me. Step exactly where I step if you want to keep your legs attached to your body."

If I wasn't worried before, his words had shoved me into full-blown paranoia. I half expected Peter Lorre to creep out of a corner, whispering, *Oh Dex, they're after me.* Like some scene out of *Casablanca.*

"Dex, now you're starting to creep me out."

He remained silent and kept walking into the room.

I followed him; it was an empty room similar to the other labs in the school, though this one had extensive runework on every surface. The door closed gently behind us and I saw a line of orange energy race along the door frame, sealing it closed.

"What's going on?" I asked as my fear factor ratcheted up a few notches. He wasn't acting overly strange—at least not overly strange for Dex—but the lurking and sealing of the door concerned me. "Why did the door lock?"

"I'll get to that in a moment," he said. "What did your Director share with you?"

After his odd behavior, his question threw me. It wasn't exactly what I was expecting.

"What do you mean?" I asked, confused. "Why are we creeping around?"

"Have you gone daft, boy?" he asked, tapping me in the forehead with a finger. "A few minutes with her and your brain stops working? What did she share with you? What did she tell you?"

"I don't understand the question," I said. "You want me to tell you what she shared with me? Why?"

"I have my reasons," he said. "There's a chance Gault got to her."

I understood the words, but the meaning behind them rocked me.

"Got to her? What do you mean got to her?"

"Focus, boy," he said, keeping his voice low. "Your Director may be compromised."

"What? No," I said, looking at the now-sealed door. "What are you talking about? That's Chi. She wouldn't work with Keeper Gault, not against me."

He gave me a hard stare.

"What if the Keeper promised the eradication of the Blood Hunters?" he asked gently. "Imagine that—your centuries-old sworn enemy, gone forever. All the vampires under her responsibility would be safe. They could freely roam the streets without fear of attack. What would you give for that kind security?"

"Keeper Gault wants to *kill* us," I said. "He wants to kill Monty and me."

"That hasn't changed, no," Dex said. "But he's not an ordinary mage. He's devious and cunning. If he can turn your Director, it makes removing you easier. She would do the hard work of handing you over. He would do the easy part of ripping the rune out of you."

"She would never do that," I said. "Not to me."

"You're letting emotion cloud your thinking, boy," he said, shaking his head. "Her first loyalty isn't to you. When was the last time you two spoke?"

"Not since Japan."

"Plenty has happened since then," he said. "As a Director, her first priority is the Dark Council. As a vampire, her loyalty must be to her kind...first. You probably come a distant third or fourth."

"I can just hand you Ebonsoul so you can jam it in deeper, thanks."

"Just being honest, boy."

"We just spoke," I said. "The feelings between us haven't changed."

"Feelings?" he asked. "You're operating on feelings? What are you, a teenager?"

"Our bond is strong."

"Are you certain?" he asked, moving over to one of the circles etched into the floor. "She tested you, didn't she?"

"Yes," I said. "She did."

"Why do you think that is?"

"She wanted to know if I had gone dark. She wanted to make sure."

"Listen very carefully to what I'm going to say to you next, boy," he said, raising a finger as he focused on the circle on the floor. "Are you paying attention?"

I nodded.

"Yes. Yes I am."

"Good. Mo and I are bonded," he said, glancing at the door again. "Through death, life, and blood. You share a similar bond with your Director, ever since she gave you that blade."

"What are you saying?"

"She didn't need to 'test' you to see if you had gone dark," he said. "All she had to do was feel for her bond to you. It would have been as clear as day if you had gone dark. You know this. Don't you?"

"I do. Then why do it?"

"You tell me."

Every option I came up with sounded bad, but I knew what we shared.

"You're wrong," I said. "If she had wanted to betray me or hand me over to Gault she could have easily taken me out when we were fighting. She clearly has the ability."

"Does she?"

"Yes. I may have upgraded, but I'm still not on her level. She could have dismantled me easily, but she didn't—even when she could have."

"Aye, a valid argument," he said. "Are you trying to convince me or yourself?"

"I don't need convincing."

"Then tell me what she said."

I told him what she had shared, about stepping down, about Esti and the impending war. I only omitted our discussion about *koi no yokan*, because Dex didn't need to know *all* of the details, even if he enjoyed torturing others with his escapades with the Morrigan.

"What do you think?" Dex said into the air. "Can he do it?"

"Who are you talking to?" I asked, looking around. "You're talking to walls now?"

The Morrigan materialized a second later on the other side of the room, nearly giving me a heart attack in the process. I took a step back and Dex shot his arm out, holding me in place.

"Boy, I told you to step where I step," he said, looking down at my feet. "A few more inches and we would be finding out if you could regrow a leg."

I looked down and saw that the heel of my foot was nearly touching one of the circles etched into the floor. I held my breath and slowly moved forward, away from the circle.

The Morrigan crossed the floor, avoiding the circles as she approached.

"Why were you skulking about?" she asked. "You looked positively foolish."

"For you, I'll play the fool any time, any place," Dex said, wagging his eyebrows at her. She rolled her eyes in response, and I felt like I had stepped into some bizarre episode of the Twilight Zone. "Besides, I don't know how to do suspicious. It goes against who I am."

"You were trying to *act* suspicious?" I asked. "That was supposed to be suspicious behavior?"

"He was supposed to act clandestine," she said. "He failed spectacularly. You, on the other hand, behaved admirably."

"I'm totally not following."

"Keeper Gault will try to use dissension to separate the catalyst from the bearer of the rune," she said. "Do you follow now?"

"Somewhat. What does this have to do with Chi?"

"The Director is a vulnerability for you," she said. "If he can sow doubt in your mind about her or about Tristan, he can use it against you."

"Divide and conquer," I said, looking at Dex. "You were acting?"

"Wasn't it apparent?" he said, glancing at the Morrigan, but pointing at me. "See, I nearly had *him* convinced."

"You nearly had me convinced that you had lost what little mind you had left," I said. "The bond between Chi and me was never in doubt."

"Good. I needed to make sure," he said. "We need to send you and my nephew back."

"Why? What happened?"

"Gault is making moves," Dex said, his expression darkening. "Not directly, not yet, but his Dark Arcanists have hit a target."

"A target...where?"

"NYTF," Dex said. "Several casualties."

"Ramirez?"

"Alive, but in critical condition at Haven," the Morrigan said. "This is a ploy to get your attention."

"It's working," I said. "How soon can we get back?"

"Within the hour," Dex said. "Ramirez wasn't unprotected. Gault's Arcanists cut through several Nightwalkers in their attempt to get to him. It appears your Director's security force was more than they reckoned."

I nodded.

If the Nightwalkers were hand-picked by Chi, Gault's Dark Arcanists would've been in for an unpleasant surprise.

"Did any of the Arcanists survive?"

"One," Dex said. "She's being held at Haven."

"We need to get to him right away," I said. "I doubt the Keeper will leave him alive long enough to reveal any details he might know."

"Which is why you're leaving within the hour," Dex said. "Go get your things ready and say your goodbyes. Your Director won't be joining you."

"Understood," I said. "Thank you both."

"You can thank us by stopping Gault," Dex said, gesturing and unlocking the door. "Mind your step and get going."

"We will speak soon, Simon," the Morrigan said as I stepped around the circles on the floor. "We still have much to discuss."

"No disrespect, but that's not exactly a conversation I'm eager to have."

She smiled, sending ripples of fear up and down my spine as I left the room.

# SIX

I left the room and headed down the hallway.

Peanut collided into me at an intersection of corridors as she turned a corner. She was dressed in her usual, white T-shirt and jeans. The blue lettering on her shirt, attributed to one Al Einstein, read: *The true sign of intelligence is not knowledge but imagination.*

It was a perfect shirt for her. I looked down and realized why her approach was so quiet. From what I could tell, she chose to go barefoot whenever possible. If this school ever had a dress code, I could foresee some difficult conversations in the future about any uniform that made footwear mandatory.

"Hello, Mr. Simon," she said, recovering quickly as she took a few steps back. "Are you going this way? Because I'm going in the same direction."

"Just heading upstairs to find Monty and Peaches," I said, playing her game. "Why don't you join me?"

"That sounds like a great idea," she answered as I continued down the hallway. As she kept pace with me, I noticed she would glance behind her every few seconds. "Uncle Dex said you would be leaving soon."

"Yes, we have to get back. There are some...situations we have to deal with."

She remained silent as we walked.

I headed to the wide stairs at the end of the corridor which led up to the ground-floor level. I casually gave her a few glances as we walked. Everything about her said she felt guilty about doing something she wasn't supposed to do while being somewhere unauthorized.

She gave me a look and a brief smile. I half expected a hand wave complete with a, "These are not the droids you're looking for," comment under her breath.

The look of extra guilt made me smile as I thought of how many times I had probably worn that same expression. As we walked, she took a moment to tie her hair back into a ponytail.

"Are you getting into trouble?" I asked, looking behind her. "Is someone chasing you?"

"Not chasing, exactly," she said as she joined me going up the stairs. "I don't get into trouble...much. Just when I'm supposed to do chores."

"Chores aren't much fun?"

"Depends on who gives them to me," she said with a mischievous smile. "Aunt Mo"—she looked around before continuing—"gives the really boring chores. Like cleaning, studying, and reading dusty old books."

"What about your Uncle Dex?"

"He gives the really fun chores," she said, lowering her voice. "I get to use my abilities and blow things up. It's awesome."

"Spoken like a true mage," I said with a laugh, and then grew serious. "It's fun to blow things up, I'm sure, but you need both. You need to study and learn how to use your abilities."

The last demonstration of the power she possessed was still fresh in my mind. Even now, her energy signature was a presence between us. She was strong, and I knew she would only grow stronger over time.

"I know, Mr. Simon," she said, serious. "Aunt Mo says her lessons will become more important as I get older. They will help me...mitigate the difficulties of not being born into a magical family. What does mitigate mean?"

"It means to make things easier, less painful," I explained. "She's probably concerned you haven't had much training and yet are very strong. That can be a dangerous combination."

She nodded. "Mr. Simon, do you have to leave right away?" she asked. "When you and Mr. Tristan are here, Aunt Mo is too busy to give me extra chores. Are you sure you can't stay for longer?"

I held back another smile at her admission that Monty's and my presence at the school was making her life lighter on the chores.

"It's just Simon," I said. "I'm sorry, we have to get back home. Some of my friends are in trouble."

"Trouble," she said pensively as she climbed the wide stairs next to me. "Big trouble?"

"Sort of, yes," I said, not wanting to share more and stress her out. "They're in trouble because of Monty and me."

"Do you need help?"

I stopped on the stairs and looked at her.

"You mean help from *you?*"

"Well, yes," she said, looking at her feet. "I know I'm young, but I can definitely help, you know. I'm still learning, but I can do more since the last time you were here."

"Really?"

"I can't tell you because it's a secret, and Uncle Dex would get mad if I shared a secret," she said, looking off to the side, torn between revealing her new abilities and keeping her word to Dex. "You shouldn't share secrets, right?"

"That's why they're called secrets," I said. "If you promised not to share, you have to keep that promise."

"Okay. I can't share what it is, but I know I can definitely help you."

"I have no doubt," I said as I continued climbing the mountain of stairs. "How about this? If Monty and I can't deal with this threat, I will make sure to get your help. That sound like a deal?"

I didn't bother explaining that if Monty and I couldn't deal with the threat, we would most likely be reduced to atom-sized particles.

"Do you promise?" she said, suddenly serious. "You give your word?"

"My word?"

"Uncle Dex says that the most important thing we have is our word," she said. "Especially for mages. I know you're not exactly a mage, but you have power, and it still counts. Do you give your word?"

I paused when we reached the ground floor.

I had answered her in an effort to keep her from worrying —but I realized then that although she looked young, she was wise beyond not only her years, but mine too.

I gave her question some thought.

"What we're about to do, the person we're going to face, is dangerous."

"I know," she said simply. "You're going to fight Keeper Guilt because you have a rune and he wants it, but it's not his to begin with, but he doesn't care, and he wants it from you and Mr. Tristan."

Mild surprise gripped me.

"His name is Gault, but yes, that's pretty much the condensed version, yes."

"And he's super strong, stronger than you."

"I think so, yes," I said, rubbing a hand through my hair. "I don't think it's going to be easy, that's for sure."

She sat on the top step and patted the stair next to her, inviting me to sit. I took the invitation because, suddenly, I felt like I was in the presence of some ancient sage.

She truly was a special child.

She clasped her hands together and looked down the stairs we had just climbed. She glanced my way before speaking.

"Sometimes, when Aunt Mo gives me chores—well, she *always* gives me chores," she said with an eye roll. "But sometimes, I don't think I'm strong enough to do some of the chores, you know what I mean?"

I could only imagine the chores the Morrigan could give a young girl gifted with the amount of power she possessed. I was certain they wouldn't be considered gentle or delicate chores—this was the Morrigan we were talking about.

"I have an idea of what you mean," I said, thinking back to Dex's lesson this morning. "Your Uncle Dex doesn't exactly take it easy on me during my lessons."

"Right, like that," she said with a nod. "They are tough because they care, but it's more than that."

"It is?"

"Whenever I feel like I can't take it anymore, I remember."

"Remember?" I asked, curious. "What do you remember?"

"I was alone. Bad people were going to take my power away," she said, lowering her voice, still looking away. "Uncle Dex and Aunt Mo stopped them. I remember that they care. They wouldn't ask me to do hard things if they didn't think I could do it. They believe in me."

"That's true," I said with a nod. "They do care."

"About you too," she said, looking at me. "What you have to do is going to be hard, right?"

"Yes, and dangerous," I said, thinking about facing a Keeper. "Real dangerous, not just for me, but everyone around me."

"But Uncle Dex and Aunt Mo believe in you," she said, getting to her feet, her moment of dispensing sage wisdom over. "I believe in you too."

"Thanks. I do appreciate that," I said, standing.

"But sometimes we need help," she said. "Sometimes we need help believing in ourselves."

I nodded.

"Sometimes...yes, sometimes we do."

"That's why you have to give me your word," she said, her voice serious. "If you forget to believe in yourself, I can remind you."

"That was some expert word-maneuvering," I said with a smile and shake of my head. "Are you sure you're not going to be some kind of mage lawyer?"

"I'm not a mage, just like you aren't a mage," she said and beamed. "Uncle Dex says I'm an outlier—a magical exception, and a rare one. So are you."

"I agree. Exceptional describes you pretty accurately."

"I know," she said, putting her hands on her hips. "Well?"

"I give you my word," I said, knowing there was no way I could outsmart her. "If I need help, I will ask you."

"Good," she said, pointing at me. "Your word is your bond. Don't forget that."

"'My word is my bond'? Was that Uncle Dex again?"

"No, that was Kai, my dragon friend," she said with a completely straight face. "He's very smart too."

"You have a...a dragon friend?" I asked, confused. "Here at the school? A real dragon?"

"Dragons are real," she replied, giving me a look of defiance. "Didn't you know?"

"Well, I know they're real," I said, thinking back to all of the dragons I had met. All of them had one thing in common —they all wanted to end me. "Are you sure that's a good idea? They can be dangerous, you know."

"Kai isn't dangerous; he's my friend, and he's not *exactly* a dragon," she clarified. "He's a drake and he can't shapeshift, at least not yet. He's still young like me, but he's still a dragon, sort of."

"If he has you as a friend, then he is a really lucky dragon," I said. "Maybe you can tell me how you met a dragon one day."

"When you visit again, I will, and then you can meet him," she said, looking away. "I have to go. Remember you gave your word!"

She dashed away and disappeared around a corner.

Monty came around the same corner and raised an eyebrow in my direction.

"Was that your doing?" he asked as he approached, glancing back the way he came. "She nearly knocked me down and then giggled profusely at the prospect of doing so."

"Are you asking if I inspire joy in young children?" I asked. "I have to say it must be my approachable charisma, unlike a certain mage I know."

"Of course," he said, pulling on a sleeve, which let me know he was concerned about something. "Perhaps you can channel some of that charisma towards Olga when we speak to her next."

"What did you do?"

"I received a message that she was less than pleased about Cecelia's recent exposure to danger," he said. "She wants to have a conversation."

"I'm not seeing how I'm part of—"

"With both of us," he finished. "She wants to speak to you, as well."

"I have nothing to do with—"

"I beg to differ, Mr. Unleash-the-Beast-and-Destroy-the-Dawnward," he said. "However, that will have to wait. Did my uncle tell you about Ramirez and the NYTF?"

"Yes. Are we sure it's Gault?"

"Fairly sure," he said. "We'll have to investigate the scene. There's also the matter of the Dark Arcanist that was apprehended. It appeared she was trying to escape."

"Escape? That makes no sense. Escape from who? Gault?"

"I don't know the details yet."

"Why can't we go back right now?" I asked. "Dex is a teleportation master. It should be easy to create a circle and send us back."

"I don't think it's that simple," he said. "This plane operates similar to the Living Library or Fordey. It seems to be in constant flux—no doubt a design by my uncle to make it difficult for the Golden Circle elders to track."

"He's really going to have to deal with them," I said. "I mean *really* deal with them."

"I hope it doesn't come to that, but I'm afraid you're right," he said. "In regards to sending us back, we have to be in some sort of alignment to particular ley lines which intersect vertices of power at specific junctions through the framework on our plane."

"Oh, is that all?" I asked, completely confused. "Can you explain that again? In English this time?"

"If I could, I would, but his explanation was beyond me," he said. "Understanding the intricacies and nuances of inter-dimensional teleportation was never my strong suit."

"Right, you were more a student of disintegration and obliteration," I said with a knowing look. "Totally understand."

"I trained as a battle mage," he said with a huff. "Interdimensional teleportation was not one of the essential subjects of study. Speaking of destruction, where is your creature?"

I searched my bond and felt him outside of the building some distance away. The direction of the sensation—which was something new—pointed to the training courtyard.

"I'm sensing him near the training courtyard," I said. "That's weird; our bond feels stronger somehow."

"It's not the bond. Most likely, it's you," he said, heading out of the building. "Roxanne sends her regards and apologizes she could not do so in person. She had to get back immediately to deal with the attack on the NYTF. She wouldn't allow anyone else to coordinate their care and my uncle facilitated her immediate return."

"I'll have to thank her," I said as we headed out of the building. "I'm sure Ramirez is in good hands. Is she safe? I mean, being back at Haven?"

"She's safe," he said. "I made a few calls and reached out to certain individuals. Haven is one of the safest and most secure locations in the city at the moment."

"That's good to know," I said, pensive. "I spoke to Michiko."

"Did you?" he asked. "It must have gone well, if you're still here to tell me about it."

"She thought I had gone *dark immortal*," I said. "We had a brief *conversation*."

"It must have been very brief since all your limbs are still attached," he said, glancing at me. "Did you explain to her that you have not gone 'dark immortal,' as you call it?"

"I did."

"Before or after she attacked you?"

"Both," I said. "She said she had to make sure, because of Izanami waking up. Had to make sure I could resist her influence."

"Grey seems to do it quite successfully," Monty said as we approached the training area. "Has Izanami tried to subjugate your will lately?"

"Nothing I can't handle," I said as we entered the courtyard. "There's more."

"Regarding Izanami?"

"No. You recall Esti? The one who lived so far out on the fringe of reality that even the Blood Hunters cut her loose?"

"I seem to recall them saving her life when you were about to end it."

"She joined something called the Sanguinary Order."

"Bloody hell, are you sure?"

"Yes," I said. "I think she still has a grudge against me."

"You did remove one of her arms," he said. "That has a way of staying with a person, deranged or not."

"I think it's more that we saved Chi," I said. "Though I'm sure the arm thing is part of it."

"I would imagine," he said. "The Sanguinary Order are fanatics. You won't be able to negotiate with them like you did with Valentina. They will not listen to reason."

"I got that," I said. "Still, I made a blood pact with Valentina. Before we go to war with this Sanguinary Order, I want to talk with Valentina."

"A prudent course of action, but Esti will not honor your blood pact," he said. "Valentina may *want* you to honor the pact."

"And I will, right up until the moment Esti tries to remove me from existence," I answered. "That would be the moment the pact is broken."

"Yes and no."

"What?"

"Esti will break the pact eventually. She has motive to do so," he said. "She hates you for removing her arm, and probably more for thwarting her plan in killing your vampire."

"But?"

"She is no longer a member of the Blood Hunters," he said. "She abandoned the Hunters to join the Order. Valentina may use that precedent to demand that you honor your pact."

"Can she do that?"

"It's a technicality, but she will try and use it," he said. "The moment you break the blood pact, the Blood Hunters will be free to act openly against the vampire community in the city."

"If they attack the vampire community, Michiko will shred them."

"She's the Director," he said, shaking his head. "There would be constraints on her attacking them directly."

I brought him up to speed on Chi's plan to step down from being Director.

"That certainly complicates things."

"You think?" I asked. "Can you imagine the Reaping Wind cutting through the Blood Hunters in the city?"

"I'd rather not," he answered. "You're going to have to convince her to take a different course of action, one that removes Esti without you breaking the blood pact."

"That sounds impossible," I said, frustrated. "She is step- ping down so she *can* hunt the enemies of vampires. I'm supposed to convince her that she shouldn't keep vampires safe?"

"You need to convince her that they would be *safer* if she didn't start a war."

"That won't work," I said. "We're going to have to remove the actual threat. We have to stop Esti before she goes on a rampage."

"Certainly. Would you like me to contact Keeper Gault and inform him we are currently busy and could he schedule the beginning of the apocalypse at a later date?"

"Your drollificence gets worse everyday," I said. "We deal with Gault first and hopefully the world will remain in one piece until we get to Esti."

"One could hope," he said as he focused on the courtyard. "How did you sense Izanami today? Was it subtle or in the heat of battle?"

"She subtly wanted me to kill Chi. I told her to shove it."

"But she didn't try to exert her will over yours?"

"No," I said. "It's all suggestions and ideas—for now, at least."

"Ebonsoul is not Darkspirit, so it may contain less of her essence. She also shares a strong bond with Grey, which may impede her ability to influence you."

"She also can't get around the bond I have with my amazing hellhound."

"There is that," he said as we arrived near the entrance to the courtyard. "You have enough bonds to prevent most entities from taking you over."

"Which is a good thing, right?"

"Depends on who you ask. In this case, if it prevents a bloodthirsty goddess from controlling you, I would say it's a very good thing."

"Again, that's because of the bond to my incredible hellhound."

"Speaking of your incredible hellhound, would that be the same hellhound that is currently about to attack the Morrigan? That hellhound?"

He pointed into the courtyard.

Peaches was going full throttle, runes on his flanks blazing bright red, as he headed for the Morrigan, who stood in the center of the courtyard.

# SEVEN

For a moment, my brain seized at the image I was seeing.

I made a move to run into the courtyard, but Monty held me back.

"That would probably be a bad idea," he said, gripping my arm. "Wait."

"Wait? Are you serious?"

"Yes. Your hellhound is virtually indestructible and he's headed towards *the Morrigan*," he explained. "Do you really think either of them is in any kind of danger?"

"Well, no," I said, stopping at the edge of the courtyard, realizing several of the training circles were active. "But still, what is this? This can't be his idea of playing."

"I doubt it's play. Look."

I turned and focused where he was pointing.

The Morrigan stood in the center of the courtyard holding a short black staff covered in red runes. I felt the energy signature of the staff from where I stood, which meant it had the potential to do massive damage, even to my hellhound.

"If she hits him with that thing, she'll kill him."

"I think hitting him is the point."

"Killing him is the point?" I asked, raising my voice. "Are you insane? I'm not going to let her hit my hellhound with that staff of destruction."

I ran forward to enter the courtyard and slammed into an invisible wall of energy which shoved me back several feet. The air around the courtyard shimmered with red energy, obscuring my vision for a few seconds before settling into transparency again.

"It would seem she has sealed the training area," Monty said, prodding the energy wall with a finger. "Fortunately for you, it's set to deterrence, not destruction."

"I noticed," I said, rubbing my face. "Why would she need a wall?"

"To prevent interruptions," he said, focusing on the interior. "They may be impervious to most kinds of damage, but we aren't. There's also the matter of children on the school grounds. If Peanut accidentally wandered in there, it could be dangerous."

"What exactly are they doing?" I asked, peering inside. "Peaches doesn't do fetch, unless he's fetching someone's arm or leg."

"Observe," he said. "This is training."

"Lethal training?"

"Lethal, perhaps, for us," he said, stepping closer to get a better look. "Probably not lethal for a hellhound of his pedigree. He is a scion of Cerberus, after all."

"I still don't like it," I said as I stepped to the edge of the courtyard, careful to avoid the energy field that closed off the space. "She could've at least asked me first, before attacking my hellhound."

"To which you would have reacted negatively," he said. "Let's see what this training entails."

"Like we have a choice," I grumbled. "She better not hurt him."

Peaches raced at the Morrigan, who swung her staff down at his head. My breath caught in my chest as I forced myself not to look away. Right before the staff connected, Peaches blinked out, appearing in the air behind her.

She sidestepped his lunge and swung at his body as he attempted to close his massive jaws on her arm. The staff missed, but the wake of energy buffeted him, sending him flying off-course to her right.

I held my breath as he raced at the far wall, letting it go when he blinked out and course-corrected, then came at her again. This time it was a series of sequential blinks, making it nearly impossible to track his angle of attack.

"I don't ever remember him doing a blink chain like that," I said, watching in awe. "That is nearly impossible to track."

"He must be maturing, applying the lessons he's learned in our battles," Monty said. "I agree. I would not want to face a hellhound that proficient in teleportation. Anticipating his next attack would be an exercise in futility."

The Morrigan swung the staff again, but was a split second too slow as he crashed into her body and bounced off. She swung an arm in an attempt at backhanding him away.

It was what he was waiting for.

He opened his massive jaws and caught her arm, clamping down on it in mid-swing. She found her balance compromised by the sudden additional weight as her arm jerked down, causing her to take a step forward.

Peaches landed with a thud, cratering the stone floor around his paws, and proceeded to shake her arm...to no effect. It would have been funny if I hadn't been so worried. He would've had a better chance trying to shake a building than move the Morrigan that way.

"That was excellent, but you'll have to do better than that

to stop me," she said calmly as she brought her staff up. "I may be immobile, but so are you."

She brought the staff down as Peaches' eyes erupted with red light and cut into the staff, shattering it to dust in her hand.

"Well done," she said with a smile. "An attack worthy of the scion of Cerberus."

He released her arm and rumbled.

"Very well. As agreed, first contact or disarm gets the prize," she said. "You managed both, and deserve an extra-large gift."

He let out a low bark which shook the courtyard.

"Do not break the courtyard," she said, pointing at him. "Dexter will be livid if we break his training area. Now, sit back and be patient."

Peaches stepped back and sat on his haunches as the Morrigan gestured, forming a huge sausage almost as long as the staff she had wielded earlier, and presented it to a very smug-looking hellhound. He chuffed, bowed his head, and took the sausage gently from her hand.

He then proceeded to walk to a corner of the courtyard where he could devour his prize without being disturbed.

The energy wall around the courtyard slowly dissipated. Soon afterward, all of the circles inside the training courtyard became dim, designating the training courtyard as inactive and safe to enter.

I took a deep breath and made sure I was calm before I approached her. She was, after all, a goddess of death. The fearsome image of the Badb Catha flashed in my memory—this was definitely a situation of think first, speak later.

The Morrigan wasn't overtly as scary as Badb Catha, but I didn't kid myself. She deliberately diminished her presence around us. If she didn't, I think we would be curled up on the floor drooling in fear at her presence.

With that thought in mind, I approached cautiously, measuring my words carefully.

"What was that, exactly?" I asked, my voice somewhere between accusatory and demanding. "That staff looked dangerous."

"For whom?" she answered, turning smoothly to face me. "He was never in any danger. At most, the staff would have given him a small jolt. He is a hellhound."

"The energy signature from that staff felt lethal."

"For you or Tristan, perhaps," she said, glancing at Peaches devouring his sausage prize. "For a hellhound of his lineage, it would barely register. Simon, are you questioning my intentions?"

"Never," I said quickly. "It was just surprising to see him attacking you."

"He wasn't *attacking* me," she said. "He was trying to tag me without being tagged in return."

"You were playing *tag?*"

"A different version, perhaps, but yes, this was training tag."

"Training tag," Monty said. "That sounds like something my uncle would devise."

"Yes," she said. "This was his idea. He felt we needed to test all of your current abilities before the coming conflict to give you a true assessment of where you stand."

"You were testing Peaches, and Dex was testing me," I asked, glancing at Monty. "I mean, I did have Michiko check to see if I had gone dark. So Roxanne—?"

"Yes," Monty said. "I'd rather *not* discuss the details."

"That fun?"

"Not in the least," he said. "She wanted to know to what extent the First Elder Rune had affected my casting. She was concerned I would be suffering deleterious effects despite the fact that I explained the rune had been divided between us two."

"That doesn't sound fun at all," I said. "Are you saying she didn't just take your word for it?"

"No, she did not," he said, and looked at the Morrigan. "Where do we stand?"

"If you three manage to work as a cohesive unit, there is a slim chance you can face, and stop, the Keeper in his pursuit of the First Elder Rune."

"I noticed you didn't say defeat him," I said. "The best we can hope for is messing up his plans?"

"He is a Keeper—that is no trivial matter," she said, glancing at me. "Tristan, your hellhound, and you are a formidable force, but to face a Keeper..."

"We can't face a Keeper," Monty said. "Is that the assessment?"

"We faced Julien," I said. "He may not be a Keeper, but he's an Archmage."

"I wouldn't exactly say we *faced off* against Julien," Monty said. "We caught him off guard, which was a feat in and of itself, but it wasn't a protracted battle."

"He was lucky to walk away from that," I said. "After what he did to Peaches—let's just say it wasn't pretty—I was ready to end him. Monty and I both were. You should've seen it."

She gave me a piercing stare followed by small smile, which chilled me.

"I did," she said. "I *was* there, if you recall."

"You were there?" I asked as the realization hit me. "Oh, you were. The other, scarier part of you."

"Simon..." Monty began, pinching the bridge of his nose. "Can you refrain from—?"

"What? I wasn't insulting her," I said. "The other part of her is much scarier than this part." I turned to her. "If I insulted you, I apologize."

"No apology is needed," she said with a nod. "Badb Catha is indeed the more fearsome aspect of my triune state. 'Scarier' fits quite appropriately."

"Do we need to do what we did with Julien to have a chance with Gault?"

"You must go beyond what you did with Julien, but there are conditions."

"Conditions?" I asked, dreading her answer. "What conditions?"

"You must face the Keeper without giving thought to your own lives," she said. "You must be willing to sacrifice everything. Any hesitation or wavering in your intent, and he will destroy you all. He will sense any doubt that enters your minds."

"Sacrifice everything," I asked pensively. "Do you think we can do this?"

"Whether or not I believe you can is irrelevant. You have to believe it."

"That sounds familiar," I said. "It's what Dex said."

She nodded.

"The manipulation of energy and the manifestation of power is, in most cases, a matter of will," she said. "It's not just will, of course, but that is a large component of its expression. Having a strong will is essential in a magic-user's life and being."

"Without it, failure is all but guaranteed," Monty said. "I remember those words from my time at the Golden Circle."

"I should hope so," Dex said from behind us, startling me. "You heard them often enough."

"You have what you need," the Morrigan said, standing next to Dex. "We will provide as much assistance as we can along the way, but you—"

"You have what Gault wants," Dex said, pointing at Monty and me. "He won't come after us, unless it's to force you two to make a move—like he's doing now with the NYTF." He stared hard at me. "He's going to apply pressure to *you* first, boy."

"That's why he went after Ramirez," I said. "He knows he's my friend."

"And he was a soft target; well, softer than others in your life," Dex said. "But make no mistake: he may have started with Ramirez, but he won't stop there. Everyone who knows you, who is important to you, is at risk."

"Do you know why he is attacking you?" the Morrigan asked. "This is not a random occurrence. There is a purpose to his strategy."

"I'm the catalyst," I said, repeating Dex's earlier words to me. "I'm the lynchpin."

"Which means you cannot let him goad you into a rash reaction," she said. "He is counting on you reacting emotionally. If you do, it will be a fatal error. He will try to force you to make this error."

"If he can take me down, everything else falls into place."

"Good to see you were paying attention," Dex said. "You know that, and Gault knows that. He's going to come at you in expected and unexpected ways. Do you understand?"

"Expect the unexpected?"

"Don't expect *anything*," Dex said with a growl. "It will narrow your focus. Deal with whatever comes with the end goal in mind."

"Stopping Gault from destroying everything?"

"I'd say that's a pretty good end goal, wouldn't you agree?"

"I would," I said. "Are you sending us back now?"

Dex nodded.

"We'll be aligned with the Haven entrance in about five minutes," he said. "Once you get there, you need to be prepared for whatever Gault throws at you. It's currently being attacked."

I saw Monty flex the muscles of his jaw and I knew he was concerned for Roxanne. Outwardly he looked calm, but I knew he was ready to get to Haven in a hurry.

"Who do you think he will send against us?"

"More like a mix of what," Dex said. "If he gets that rune"—he pointed at Monty and me—"you lose. If you lose, we *all* lose."

"Is Haven under attack?" I asked. "When did this happen?"

"As of two minutes ago," Dex said. "I don't have the details yet, but it's probably due to the Dark Arcanist that was captured—she seems important—and your friend, the NYTF Director."

"They would attack a whole facility just to get to Ramirez?"

"No, boy," Dex said, his voice grim and placing a hand on my shoulder. "Gault would attack a whole facility to get to *you*. Are you seeing it now?"

"Ramirez is an excuse to draw us...to draw *me* out?"

"Exactly," Dex said with a nod. "To get the *both* of you somewhere he can attack with ease."

"Then aren't we just walking into a trap?"

"Aye, but it's not a trap if you *know* it's a trap. Besides, if you don't go to Haven, Gault will level the place. We can't have that."

"Still seems like a trap, even if I know it's a trap. The only difference is that now I know I'm walking into a trap. Doesn't change the trappiness of the situation."

"Trap or not, Ramirez and Roxanne are there, along with hundreds of innocents."

"Innocents who will die if we don't stop them," Monty said, focusing on Dex. "Did you contact them? The backup?"

"It took some wrangling and I now owe some favors, but

yes, I made contact," Dex said. "They're solid for the work that lies before you."

"How far out are they?"

"They should be waiting for you once you arrive," Dex said. "I'll try and place you as close as possible to the action, but this method of teleportation is still untested. There may be some deviation from the target location."

"We're using an untested method of teleportation?" I asked warily. "That sounds dangerous. Don't you have a tested method you can use?"

"Not from here, I don't," Dex said with a grin. "Don't worry. Have I ever steered you wrong?"

"Are we talking about today or just in general? Because there was a certain orb on a plane, followed by facing a scary axe-mace. Then there was the time—"

"No one likes a smartass," Dex said with a growl. "You're still here, aren't you?"

"I have no idea how, some days."

"Quit your bellyaching and focus," Dex answered. "You will both be entering a live-fire situation. Make your way to the ICU-R. Ramirez and the Dark Arcanist will be there. Find them and teleport out."

"For this to happen, we need to be on the same floor and in the same wing as Ramirez and the Dark Arcanist," Monty said. "Will that be possible?"

"I'm the best," Dex said, "But I'm not perfect. I'll do what I can; you make sure you're ready to step into instant carnage."

"Instant carnage?" I asked, concerned. "Could we have the slow-building kind? Instant carnage sounds lethal."

"Because it is," Dex said with another grin. "If you wanted slow-building carnage, you are living the wrong life, boy. By now, you should be used to this."

"I will *never* get used to this, but at least I'm understanding that this is my life," I said. "How bad is this instant carnage?"

"Gault has his Dark Arcanists, but there's more."

"More? More what? More Dark Arcanists?"

"More like creatures you wouldn't want to face on a good day," Dex said. "And this is *not* a good day. There are rumors of the Keeper using thralls."

"Thralls? What exactly are thralls? He has some Igors running around ready to attack us?"

"You need to get out more, boy. Thralls are nasty things," Dex said with a grimace. "Gault uses them as a horde, so be careful not to get overwhelmed. Oh, and they're poisonous. Do not engage them in close quarters."

"Poisonous thralls," I said, dreading running into these creatures. "Well, they sound like fun. That's it? Dark Arcanists and thralls? Not that I'm complaining—I'm good with Dark Arcanists with a side of poison thrall horde."

"Boy, this is you two we're discussing," Dex said, pointing at us. "Do you really think it would only be Dark Arcanists and thralls?"

"Yes?" I said, hopeful. "For once, can it just be something we can barely manage?"

"He'll send ogres, and if you're in luck and he's holding true to form, expect a trollgre or two," Dex said. "You're not there to fight them. Get your friend and the Dark Arcanist, and get out. You leave Roxanne and your backup there to deal with the creatures."

"We're leaving Roxanne? Seriously?"

"Yes," Monty said, his face dark. "She can't leave."

"You're not serious—we're going to leave her to face ogres, Dark Arcanists, thralls and maybe a trollgre or two?" I asked, turning to him in disbelief. "Are you insane? It's Roxanne. She's—"

"The Director of Haven, and responsible for *all* the patients there."

"I know, but—"

"She is also a powerful sorceress," Monty said. "Do you really think I haven't had this conversation with her?"

"She said she wasn't leaving?" I asked, still surprised. "You couldn't convince her?"

"Precisely," he said, his words clipped. "Did you manage to convince *your* vampire to stay here, where it was safe?"

"Are you kidding?" I said. "I may be insane, but I'm not suicidal. She went back as soon as she was sure I hadn't gone all *dark immortal*. I wasn't going to be able to stop her, no matter how she feels about me."

"Then you understand Roxanne's position," Monty said. "Haven is her responsibility. She will not abandon them, nor will she be convinced to do so by anyone. Not even *me*."

"Understood. So this is an extraction," I said. "We go in, get Ramirez and the Dark Arcanist, and get the hell out of Dodge."

"Aye," Dex said with a nod. "This is an opening move by Gault. He wants to see how far he can push before he confronts you directly. He will be looking for advantages and weaknesses. Try not to show him any."

"This totally sucks. He only has to succeed once," I said. "We have to succeed in stopping him every single time."

"Welcome to being a hero," Dex said. "It's a thankless, difficult job, but if you don't stand in his way—if *we* don't stand in his way—he wins and we all lose."

"We won't lose," I said. "We can't."

"Well, it's not like we'll be around to moan about it if you do," Dex said with a crooked grin as he gestured, forming a large, green circle under us. "Call your hound."

I looked over to the corner to call out to my hellhound,

but Peaches was already by my leg. I rubbed his massive head as he chuffed at me and sat on his haunches inside the circle. He managed to do this without an attempt at knocking one of my hips out of joint, which surprised me.

*<Hey, boy. Good job on beating the Morrigan at training tag. I was worried there for a second.>*

*<I am the Mighty Peaches. I am too fast for her to see me. She is very strong. I hit her with my head, but she didn't move. She must eat large amounts of meat.>*

*<I saw. Why didn't you unleash your bark?>*

*<She told me the old bird man would be angry if I broke his play space. If I spoke, it would have broken everything, and she wouldn't make me meat.>*

*<Can she speak with you?>*

*<Yes, the same way she speaks with you.>*

I internally rolled my eyes at the hellhound sarcasm.

*<You know what I mean—can she speak with you the way I do?>*

*<No, only we can speak this way. She is not my bondmate.>*

*<Just checking. You two seemed to be on the same page during that training tag session.>*

*<I am very intelligent. It's part of being mighty. I speak this way so you can understand me. When you become mighty, you will learn to speak better.>*

Nothing like being called less intelligent by your hellhound to lift your spirits.

*<Thanks, I think.>*

*<You will get stronger. Then you can be mighty like me.>*

*<I know you are. She just seemed much stronger than you. Were you holding back?>*

*<I only had to hit her or break her stick. Then she would make me meat. I wasn't trying to hurt her. She is a nice, scary lady.>*

*<That stick she was using looked like it would hurt.>*

*<It wouldn't hurt me. I am the Mighty Peaches.>*

<She's still plenty strong.>

<You could be just as strong as she is, if you ate more meat.>

<I think there's a little more to it than that. She's a goddess; her power doesn't come from eating meat.>

<My power comes from eating meat and from my bondmate. I will need to eat soon. My stomach is getting empty.>

<What? You just ate a massive sausage almost as long as my leg.>

<Yes, but I had to use my energy to get it. I'm a growing hellhound. It's not easy to be the Mighty Peaches. You need to increase my meat. Can we go to the place?>

<I'll give that serious thought. Are you ready to go?>

<Wherever you go, I go. I'm ready.>

<We have to face a Keeper. This is going to be harder than Julien.>

<You need to eat more meat. If you do, we can be stronger. Strong enough to face a goddess or a Keeper. Strong enough to face anyone.>

I was unsure if he was just pushing his perpetual meat agenda, or if there was a deeper truth to his words. I would have to find out more about this battle form he had, and see if I could discover a way to activate it.

If it increased his strength and mine along with his, it was worth seeing how it could be activated for when we faced beings bent on destroying us and well, everything.

I doubted it had anything to do with eating more meat, but I wondered if the meaning behind the meat conversations was more about my growing in strength and power, using what little ability I had.

"The Haven passage is open," Dex said. "The next alignment will be at the Moscow in twenty-four hours. Make sure you manage to stay alive at least until then. I'll bring some help."

"Help would be good," I said. "Can you bring someone stronger than Gault? Several someones would be even better. That would be very helpful."

"Don't count on it," he said, serious. "But I'll see what I can do. Get ready."

With a gesture, the runic symbols in the circle came to life as a green mist surrounded us. We watched the School of Battle Magic vanish from sight.

# EIGHT

We stepped into a warzone.

Screams and roars filled the air around us. The walls were blasted and broken in several sections with scorch marks where orbs had hit. We made our way around the parts of the floor that were still intact as we moved down the hospital corridor.

From what I could see, we were definitely in Haven—if the facility had been under siege by a small army bent on destroying the place.

"They've been here longer than a few minutes," I said, raising my voice and looking around. "Are they trying to destroy the place?"

"Yes," Monty said, raising a shield and deflecting several orbs headed our way. "It would appear my uncle's assessment of the time of attack is off. I wonder if it has anything to do with the school being off-plane creating a temporal displacement?"

"I wonder if we could put some distance between us and them?" I asked before he lost himself in professor mode. "They don't seem happy to see us."

"It does seem they're trying to get down this corridor."

"Noticed that, did you?" I said, looking around us for an exit. We only had one way to go—back. Behind us was a small open area that led off to another corridor. "Nice of Dex to put us right in their path."

"My uncle does believe in being efficient," he said, creating another shield and sending violet orbs down the corridor. "We need to move."

We dashed down the center of a corridor decorated with white and pastel blue tiling. The walls, floor, and ceiling were covered with subtle runic symbols. A red haze of energy filled the air, cutting down the visibility all around us. We were definitely in the magical side of Haven.

I sensed an energy spike and ducked, then dodged to the side as a black orb flew by my head and punched a hole into the wall behind me. Monty unleashed several more violet orbs down the corridor as I dove for cover behind a shattered receptionist desk.

The corridor we currently inhabited led to an open reception area behind us. I turned to look down the corridor where the black orb came from, and at the end of the corridor I saw a sight that chilled my blood.

Two ogres were lumbering our way.

"Any chance those two ogres headed our way are lost?"

"None," Monty said as he gestured. "They look decidedly displeased."

"Probably the food," I said, making sure Grim Whisper was loaded with entropy rounds. "Hospital food will make an ogre out of anyone."

"Well done," Monty said with a nod as he gestured, "though I doubt Roxanne will appreciate the slight to Haven's culinary offerings."

"I'll apologize when I see her," I said. "Can we stop those things now?"

"Working on it."

The two ugly ogres with death on their minds wore an expression of maximum anger as they headed our way. To be fair, that was their resting "maim you" face. Ogres, at least in my experience, never had a pleasant expression on their faces. It was always a grimace of anger and hatred, baring their teeth in a display of lethal intent.

"It's not just ogres," I said, backing up farther. "What the hell?"

"My uncle did warn us," Monty said as he glanced behind us. "Where are they?"

Behind the ogres, I saw a group of Dark Arcanists—Verity mages who looked very much like the mages Monty and I faced before. Their hands were enveloped in black energy, and they felt stronger than normal Verity mages. Each of them had formed black-and-red orbs of energy which looked unfriendly; I counted at least five of them, which felt like a small amount, until I noticed the bodies on the floor.

There were many bodies in different states of agony. From the wounds I saw, most of them didn't look like they were going to make it.

Normally, seeing this many wounded would make perfect sense—we were in a hospital, after all—except these bodies were not laying comfortably in beds, being treated. These were the broken bodies of Dark Arcanists and other creatures I had not seen before.

They reminded me of shamblers, except they were less on the zombie side and more on the "shred your face off" side. There were other bodies as well—Haven Security.

From what I could make out of the uniforms, Elias' people had fought and died here. I noticed at least a dozen of them all over the corridor. Haven Security had made a stand here, and taken out a large part of their group. There were at least a dozen or more Dark Arcanists on the floor.

"Elias' people must've cut through their numbers," I said, "before they were overrun."

"They had to abandon this position before falling back," Monty said, glancing at the fallen security personnel. "The horde was most likely the reason."

"They were rolled over by those things," I said, looking at the creatures down the corridor. They stood out among the ogres and Dark Arcanists. These creatures were smaller and disfigured, their bodies bent, and their faces twisted in pain and rage. "They seem less happy than the ogres."

"They are born of rage and anguish, driven mad by pain, and then unleashed on unsuspecting targets," Monty said, his voice low and angry. "I haven't seen them in ages and had hoped to never see them again."

"You know, you have some of the scariest memories of anyone I know."

"You live long enough, and all your memories turn to ash, filled with death and despair," Monty said. "Those creatures used to be human...once."

"Can we dial back the death and despair until after I've had my coffee?" I said, focused on the screeching creatures. "You said they were human?"

"Once," he said as we put more distance between us and the creatures. "No longer."

"What exactly are they?" I asked as he unleashed another barrage of orbs at the approaching ogres. "They look like shamblers, but worse."

"Those are thralls. To unleash this many is an indication that Gault is serious," Monty said. "Unleashing thralls is no small matter."

"The thralls mean he's serious? Really? The thralls?"

"Yes. They are incredibly hard to control, destroying everything in their path," he answered. "Releasing this many is reckless."

I stared at him for a second.

"Oh, I thought the ogres and the Darkanists got the serious message across clearly," I said. "I didn't realize it was the concentration of *thralls* that pushed this situation into serious territory."

"Your humor, as usual, disappoints," he said. "We need a way to stop those ogres before they reach us."

"Before they reach us is good," I said, firing Grim Whisper. "I'm all for stopping them before they reach us."

My rounds punched into several shields before I realized the Darkanists were deflecting my shots from reaching the ogres.

"The Darkanists are stopping my rounds," I continued, holstering Grim Whisper. "Can you stop the thralls?"

"The what? Nevermind," he said, quickly waving my words away, "I can create a lattice network, but it won't be perm—"

A roar filled the floor.

"*That* was not an ogre," I said, as we kept backing up. "Monty?"

"Bloody hell," he said, gesturing and throwing up five golden lattices of power that blocked the hallway before he joined me in backing up. "That won't hold them for long. Where are they? They were supposed to key in on our signature."

"What was that roar?" I asked, looking through the lattices, behind the ogres, Darkanists, and thralls. "Who? Who was supposed to key in on our signature?"

"That roar was a trollgre," he said, looking around. "We need to locate the ICU-R. Ramirez and the Dark Arcanist that was apprehended will be there. Where exactly did my uncle drop us, and why isn't our backup here?"

"I'm not seeing any backup," I said, pointing at the mob of gruesome in front of us. "All I see is a world of pain and death that wants to get from way over there to here, where we are."

"We must be close to Ramirez and the Dark Arcanist," Monty said. "Or they wouldn't be trying to get here. Roxanne is some distance away."

"You can sense her through all this?"

"Of course," he said matter-of-factly. "She's approximately eight hundred meters south of our position—that way."

He pointed back across the corridor through the group of creatures and Darkanists, all of whom were working their way toward us. One of the lattices had been destroyed and the ogres were making short work of the second layer.

"Tell me we don't have to go through them to get to Roxanne."

"No, we'll take the long way around," he said. "Whatever you do, don't let the thralls wound you or your creature. Death at their hands is a long, agonizing, ordeal. The runic poison in their bodies is almost impossible to stop."

"Even for my curse?"

"Are you willing to find out?"

"That's going to be a no."

"Good. Don't let them wound, scratch or bite you."

"Bite?" I asked. "You're joking?"

"I'm deadly serious, Simon," he said. "Use your gun, not your blade. Do not let them get close. Put them down if they get past my barriers."

"Are you sure they aren't related to shamblers?"

"Positive," he said as I peered through his lattices which were still holding. He moved over to a map that was attached to one of the walls nearby. "ICU-R is behind us—good. At least we're in the right wing of Haven."

The sounds from the thralls were reaching nails on a chalkboard territory to an extreme degree as they clawed at the lattices.

"Why are they screeching like that?" I asked, rubbing a finger in my ear. "That sound cuts right through you."

"Thralls do not possess the power of speech," Monty said, glancing down the corridor. "It's the first aspect of humanity that's lost."

I looked down the corridor as the ogres continuously pounded their fists against Monty's lattice. Behind the ogres stood the Darkanists, which had grown to a group of ten. Behind them, I saw the gnarled and bent figures of the thralls which were surprisingly *not* attacking the Dark Arcanists.

"Why aren't those thralls chomping on the Darkanists?"

Monty peered down the corridor and narrowed his eyes.

"They're being controlled by one of the Dark Arcanists. That one," he said, pointing to a taller figure behind all of the Dark Arcanists. "He has them all tethered—they will do as he commands."

I looked at the Darkanist Monty singled out, and the Darkanist nodded his head at me. I made a note to remember his face. It was always good to remember the people who want to unleash death in your direction. The only polite thing to do was to return the favor.

I returned the nod and added a signature single-finger expression of diplomacy and tact. He laughed, but I could see the anger and determination filling his eyes.

Mages. So easy to rile.

Behind the thralls, towering over everything, I saw the trollgre. It locked eyes with me and grinned, or at least I think it was a grin. Trollgres made ogres look absolutely handsome in comparison. Whoever thought it was a good idea to create that hybrid was beyond deranged and needed help.

This trollgre looked like it had been smashed in the face repeatedly with a shovel, which was then exchanged for a sledgehammer to finish off the job. Despite the stomach-turning face, it was the sharp intelligence in its eyes that drove a large spike of fear into me.

This wasn't some mindless creature.

It stared at me and I noticed it did the same thing I had just done with the Darkanist. It was studying my face and archiving my features for future limb-ripping reference.

While the ogres worked on the remaining lattice barriers, the trollgre waited in the back, arms crossed. It looked almost bored, but I knew. Worse, it knew that I knew as it grinned at me. Sooner or later, they were going to get through the obstacle that the lattices presented, and then it was coming for us.

For me.

A fist punched through the wall down the corridor behind me.

I whirled, drawing Grim Whisper as Ebonsoul formed instantly in my opposite hand. Peaches immediately dropped into a maim-and-shred stance, unleashing a menacing growl. The arm pulled back and wrecked more of the wall. This was followed by the crash of a huge battle-axe that removed what remained of the destroyed wall.

I recognized the large, double-bladed axe covered in dark energy as an undercurrent of fear and destruction filled the corridor we stood in. Even the ogres behind us paused in their attack as the axe cleared out the rest of the wall.

They stared down the corridor past me, focusing on the axe as it made quick work of the wall. For a few brief seconds they were frozen, caught in the cloud of fear created by the weapon.

Then the trollgre roared, said something in a guttural language I had no hope of understanding, and pounded a fist against the wall, leaving a large crater as the runes in the wall flashed with violet energy. The ogres snapped out of it and began attacking the lattice again, this time with a renewed determination.

The fact that the trollgre could damage a rune-enhanced wall meant either it had some serious runic power or else it was immune to the power of the runes in the walls. That wall should have withstood the fist with little to no damage, yet this trollgre nearly put a hole in it.

That was not good.

"Monty," I asked tentatively, "is it supposed to be able to do that?"

I pointed at the crater in the wall.

"Do what?" he asked impatiently as he turned to look up the corridor at the trollgre. "Well, that's interesting."

"Interesting?" I said. "That wall is covered in runes. How did it do that?"

"That trollgre must be runically enhanced," Monty explained, turning again to the activity behind us. "It could explain why the ogres fear it. It's much stronger than a typical trollgre. I suggest we avoid engaging it as much as possible."

"Great suggestion. I was just about to ask it down to the Randy Rump for a large mug of coffee," I snapped. "Good thing you warned me. Avoid it as much as possible? That's your suggestion?"

"We are not here to do battle, Simon," Monty said, approaching the destroyed wall. "We are here to extract our targets, nothing more. This force is not here to fight us. It's why they have redoubled their efforts to tear my lattices down. Aside from their fear of the trollgre, they have to stop us. At least, that was the command."

It did seem the ogres were more scared of the trollgre than the axe that had created a new passageway for us. I could understand why. The trollgre was right behind them, promising pain—or worse, if the fist in the wall meant anything.

The scary axe was way over here, on the other side of the lattices and not much of a threat to the ogres, at least not yet. The energy and feeling of dread coming off the axe was familiar, until it finally clicked.

Stormchaser.

"You know, they certainly look like they want to do more than delay us," I said, looking down the corridor again. "I'm getting a major 'rip off their heads' vibe from those ogres."

"Killing us would be, technically speaking, delaying us," he said. "I don't think they make a distinction in the method. The end result is the same."

"Thanks for clarifying," I said. Then it clicked: he had understood whatever the trollgre had screamed. "Wait a minute, you speak trollgre?"

"I dabble," he said, his voice low and grim. "The command was to stop us and hold us here for someone or something. I couldn't quite catch the last part, but whatever is coming is going to be much worse than a trollgre."

"What could possibly be worse than—?"

"Strong," a familiar voice called out. "Have you worked on your battlecry?"

Nan stuck her head through the wrecked wall with a huge grin on her face. Wearing her black combat armor, she towered over us. Her energy signature radiated into the surrounding area, promising death to all who would stand before her, before she looked past us at the assorted group of walking pain. As she did so, her expression darkened.

"My battlecry?" I asked surprised. "What are *you* doing here?"

"Come with me if you want to live," she said, motioning to us to follow her. "Now."

"There you are," Monty said as we made our way through the wall. "What happened?"

"This area was sealed behind wards and runes by the

sorceress," she said. "Then she sensed you stroll right into the middle of that nightmare back there. We had no clear path to you, so I had to make one. I can take you to your friend and the captured enemy. Talk later, run now."

She took off at a dead run, with us behind her.

# NINE

We ran through several walls with Nan-designed holes in them.

"Roxanne is going to be so pissed at this damage," I said under my breath as we ran. "Nan literally punched her way to us."

"The damage is the least of our concerns at the moment," Monty said. "How long has that attacking force been in the facility?"

"An hour, give or take a few minutes," Nan said. "Haven Security encountered them first, and, well—"

"We saw," I finished. "It didn't end well for them."

"They fell in battle," she said. "They died honorably. A warrior's death is the least any of us can ask for."

"Where is the rest of the security force?" Monty asked. "Are they nearby?"

"They are engaging the enemy on several fronts in the runic wing," she said as we kept moving. "Elias is a formidable leader, as competent as any Valkyrie, and fearsome in battle. I look forward to fighting by his side again."

If I didn't know better, I would've said Nan had a slight crush on Elias. Since I enjoyed breathing, and having all my body parts *attached* to my body, I neglected to share my thoughts—it probably had something to do with the large double-headed axe she swung around as we raced through the walls.

"I don't think Roxanne is going to appreciate the renovation effort," I said, glancing behind us as we moved. "This is some major destruction."

"Couldn't be helped," Nan called out from the front. "We needed a direct route to you that bypassed most of the defenses."

"If you bypassed the defenses, doesn't that mean you just created a way for the ogres behind us to bypass those same defenses?"

"Up to a point," she said. "Once they get past the mage's barrier back there, they'll be able to follow us—which is why we're running and not taking a pleasant stroll through the destruction, Strong."

"Up to a point? What does that mean, up to a point?"

"There," Nan pointed ahead of us into a swirling orange, yellow, and violet vortex. "We need to get through that."

I looked where she pointed, and fear stopped me in my tracks.

"That's not a void—"

"No," Monty said. "It's worse, so much worse. That's a negating vortex. I haven't seen one of those since the war."

"A what?"

"I have them," Nan called out to the air. "Stand back."

"If you combined a void vortex and an entropic dissolution, you would get that," Monty said, pointing at the swirling mass of orange, yellow, and violet energy that whirled in front of us. "How is Roxanne keeping it contained? It should be devouring everything around it right now."

"Roxanne cast this?" I asked, surprised at Monty's words. "Isn't that thing dangerous?"

"It's a banned cast," Monty said, his voice dark. "Even during the war, this was only used as a last resort. It's a horrifically lethal attack, and nearly impossible to undo."

"And Roxanne created this?" I asked, examining the vortex from a distance. The suction of the energy signature was overwhelming. I felt its tug as it rotated slowly in front of us. If I stepped closer, I was certain it would pull me in. I took a few extra steps back. "Can she control it? Or are we going to be running from a negating vortex?"

Nan pointed Stormchaser at the vortex, and its rotation slowed down.

"I didn't even think she possessed the knowledge to do this," he said as the vortex parted, creating a path for us. "Whatever you do, do not touch the sides of the vortex. It will undo you instantly and completely."

"This is not your sorceress' doing," Nan said, her voice tight with strain. "The Midnight Echelon is not without power of its own."

"You did this?" I asked, surprised. "How?"

Nan silently thrust a finger forward through the passage that had opened. Her message was clear. We ran through the open vortex passage with Nan bringing up the rear. She slashed down with Stormchaser once we were clear, and the vortex closed, increasing in speed again as it blocked our rear.

"Of course," Monty said. "This is a battlefield cast. It makes sense the Valkyries could create something like this, though I never thought I would live to see another one."

Nan took point again and led us down another corridor.

Behind us, the negating vortex blocked the entire corridor and continued expanding. I glanced at it one more time before I caught up with the rest of the group.

"Is that thing going to continue expanding?"

"Yes," Nan said, stopping as she examined a wall. "It will cut off the entire runic wing of Haven."

"What about the patients—?"

"The runic wing has been evacuated," Nan said, pausing to rub Peaches' massive head. "Well met, Mighty Peaches."

Peaches gave her a rumble in response.

"All of the runic wing is empty?" Monty asked. "No collateral damage?"

"Your Director said you would ask," Nan answered as she pressed certain sections of the wall in front of her. "The runic wing has been evacuated; those patients were teleported to safety."

"She's not my—"

"Yes, she is," Nan said, cutting him off. "She was the one who sensed you, before any of us knew you were even in the facility. That goes beyond her abilities. She is as bonded to you as you are to her. Do you deny it?"

"I do not," Monty said.

"You'd be a fool to do so," Nan said as a group of runes formed a portal in the wall. She stepped through and motioned for us to follow. "This way."

We stepped through the portal into what I could only describe as an extra-large hospital room. Several beds of assorted sizes were situated around the floor. Beside the portal, I saw another of the Midnight Echelon: Braun.

She wasn't as tall as Nan—I don't think any of the Midnight Echelon were as tall or dangerous as Nan—but she came close. Braun nodded to me as the portal closed behind us.

She placed her right fist over her heart and bowed slightly to Nan, who returned the gesture. Then she looked behind us as if expecting someone else.

"You didn't let them follow you?" Braun asked. "Are they coming?"

"They'll be here soon enough," Nan said with a small chuckle as she thumbed a finger in our direction. "First we have to get them and their targets out of the facility."

"But we will get to go back, yes?"

I stared at Braun in disbelief.

"You *want* to go back?" I asked. "There's a trollgre and an assortment of nasties back there."

"I know," Braun said, walking over to my hellhound. "Well met, Mighty One."

Peaches rumbled in response.

"And you *want* to go back?"

"Yes," Braun said, shooting Nan a look. "Someone hasn't been sharing, taking all the fights for herself. We don't even have the full Echelon here. It's just me and Nan. I haven't punched anything in over ten minutes."

"Battle is what they live for," Roxanne said as she appeared in a doorway. "Hello, Tristan." She gave him a long look as she stepped close to him before turning in my direction. "Simon, I've stabilized your friend, but you still have to be careful with him during the transport."

She was dressed in gray combat leathers and carried a bag full of medical instruments. I noticed the group of angry black-and-red orbs that hovered lazily around her head as she moved.

"What are those?" I said, pointing at the orbs. "They look—"

"Deadly, because they are," she finished, her voice laced with concern. She turned to Braun. "Can you help them with the extraction? Once that's done, we will begin housekeeping."

"Housekeeping?" I asked. "You're going to—?"

"Make sure you get out of Haven in one piece," she said. "Braun, please bring the Director of the NYTF. We can cast the circle here."

Braun nodded while Nan took her spot by the wall where the portal had formed.

"Are you certain you need to do this?" Monty asked. "The Midnight Echelon is more than capable. They are—"

"Not responsible for Haven. I am," Roxanne said. "We will remove the intruders without disrupting the greater wards around Haven."

"I would feel better if you just let them deal with this threat."

"I know," she said. "You know I can't and won't allow that. I am the Director of this facility. To attack Haven, a place of healing, means this Keeper has no limits. I will not allow this attack to go unanswered. Haven will remain standing."

"Monty, the longer we're here, the more we place Haven in danger," I said. "Let's extract Ramirez and the Darkanist, and get away from here. She's going to be okay. She has Nan and Braun—if anything, those ogres should be the ones worried."

Nan nodded from where she stood at the wall.

"I understand your argument, rationally," Monty said. "However, that trollgre gives me pause. What it did to that wall...it's resistant to the runes."

"Then we should drag it with us, don't you think?" I said. "Let's not leave it here. The sooner we go, the sooner it follows. Roxanne can handle herself."

"I'm aware," Monty said, turning to Roxanne. "I would never impugn your ability to defend yourself or Haven. I'm just—"

She placed a finger on his lips.

"I know," she said, "but you need to go...now. The Valkyries and I will deal with the threat. You have greater concerns to worry about at the moment."

"Greater than your well-being?"

"Yes, Tristan," she said, her voice suddenly hard. "Gault

wants to destroy everything. You and Simon have to stop him. You must focus."

"Monty..." I began.

"I know," he snapped, before taking in a deep breath and letting it out slowly. "I know."

Braun entered the room with an unconscious Ramirez in a wheelchair. Behind her followed a slim woman with her hands cuffed in front of her, the cuffs covered in runic symbols were giving off a pale orange glow.

The woman was young, somewhere in her mid-twenties, with short, black hair. She wore the mageiform of an Arcanist: a dark suit with a dark shirt and some red accent. In this case, it was a red tie with runework along its length. The suit was an inferior version of Monty's Zegna bespoke suits.

The cuffs she wore pulsed a brighter orange with every step she took.

"What are those?" I asked, looking at the cuffs.

"Inhibitors," Roxanne said. "She has agreed to cooperate, which means Gault will almost certainly try to end her life."

"Why?"

"Why will he end her life?" Roxanne asked incredulously, "or why is she cooperating?"

"The second one."

"You can ask her yourself after you leave," Roxanne said, placing her hands together and forming a large, red circle on the floor beneath us as she and the Midnight Echelon stepped back. She looked up for a few seconds, before moving her hands with urgency. "You need to go now. They're coming."

"Let them help you," Monty said. "That is why they are here."

"I have every intention of doing so," Roxanne said. "Now. Go stop Gau—"

The wall next to Nan erupted in a blast of energy and

formed a ragged portal as Roxanne activated the circle under us. I saw an ogre sail into Nan only to be batted away by her fist. The other ogre roared as it crashed through the portal and onto the floor.

Monty and I took several steps forward only to be stopped by the energy at the edge of the circle. Monty began gesturing, but his symbols vanished before he could finish the cast.

"What did you do?" he demanded. "Drop this barrier immediately."

"I knew you wouldn't be able to refrain from helping," Roxanne said, "so I took a few precautions."

"You activated Haven's failsafes?"

"Yes."

"Which ones?"

"The ones you inscribed."

"Which failsafes?"

"The ones that would prevent you from leaving that circle," she said. "We all have our part to play, Tristan. Go do what only you and Simon can do. We will handle this."

"No!" he said. "Don't do this."

"It's already done."

The thralls began pouring in from the portal in the wall, screeching as they climbed over one another to gain entrance. Behind the thralls, I could see the trollgre pushing its way forward, tossing thralls and Darkanists aside.

Braun leapt into the mob and began crushing thralls, flinging their dead bodies to the sides, as Nan engaged the trollgre. It roared as she approached and unleashed a fist at her face.

She laughed as she slipped past the enormous hand and buried her axe into its ribs. The trollgre barely registered the weapon in its side, as it swung a tree trunk of an arm at her head. Nan blocked the arm with a forearm and pried her axe loose, doing as much damage as possible as she pulled it free.

It kicked forward and connected, sending her back as Braun leapt into the gap, slamming an elbow into the trollgre's head. It roared again as the orbs around Roxanne crashed into its back and exploded.

Braun buried a fist into its midsection and it bared its teeth at her. She grinned back, letting out a roar of her own before wrapping her other arm around its neck, lifting the trollgre off the floor and throwing it over her shoulder...at Nan—who was waiting with axe in hand.

Monty crouched down to examine the circle, looking for a way to get out, but he quickly realized it was futile. He was trying to undo his own work and knew he didn't have time. He got to his feet as Peaches rumbled and growled by my side.

<What's wrong, boy?>

<I can help them. The angry man wants to help them.>

<I know, but we have to go. This is a small part of a bigger fight. If we stay, we'll make things worse.>

<We'll make things worse by helping?>

<This is not our fight. Not yet. Our fight is with someone else.>

Monty gestured one more time and failed as the circle around us increased in brightness. With a gesture, Roxanne formed more orbs and unleashed them around her, ending several thralls and Darkanists where they stood.

As the circle intensified, I was able to see one of the ogres had fallen and the second one looked like it was in trouble as Braun pounded on it mercilessly.

Monty placed a hand on the wall of energy keeping us inside the circle. I had no doubt that given enough time, he could find some way around the defenses.

Roxanne glanced back once at Monty, and mouthed, *Go,*

as she slashed an arm through the air. Monty looked on, gesturing futilely one last time as the circle blazed fully to life.

Haven disappeared a moment later.

# TEN

The five of us arrived at our space in the Moscow.

Sunlight spilled in through the windows, bathing the interior in a golden light. The sudden silence that greeted us was a mild shock compared to the sounds of fighting we had just left.

I pushed Ramirez into the reception area and looked around. Those first few seconds of being home were always the best. It was a momentary feeling of relief and comfort—one quickly followed by the fact that we weren't going to be staying long. I really needed a vacation.

I looked at the Darkanist and knew her presence here meant we would have to leave soon. She worked for Gault, and I had a feeling she was more than she appeared to be.

I headed to the kitchen as Monty crossed the reception area, frustration and anger coming off of him in waves. I knew he wanted to go back immediately. It's what I would have wanted, too, if I had left Chi to face off against those monsters.

I would've been wrong, but that didn't mean I wouldn't try to find a way to go back. Monty being a mage meant he had a better chance of creating that way back, but I figured if Roxanne had activated failsafes, it wasn't going to be easy for him to create a teleportation circle to Haven.

He gestured and created a circle, which evaporated a few seconds later.

Ramirez stirred in the chair. I motioned for my hellhound to stay put, not that it looked like he was going to follow me, and wheeled the sleeping Ramirez into a small room off the reception area. The room held a sizable daybed that would be comfortable enough for him, so I moved him from the chair and laid him down where he could sleep in relative peace while Monty and I discussed the situation.

"She has blocked Haven's runic wing," he said as he tried to gesture again. "Why would she do such a foolish thing?"

"She doesn't want us there—and when I say us, I really mean *you*."

"An astute and pointless observation," he snapped. "I know she doesn't want us there. She's also facing a trollgre, thralls, and Darkanists."

He glanced at our guest as he said that last word.

I took a deep breath and did my best to remain calm. I didn't think Roxanne was in danger. If I had to bet on who would walk away from Haven today, my money was on Roxanne and the Midnight Echelon.

There was no scenario where I would want to face any of the Echelon, or Roxanne for that matter, in a fight to the death. There was also Elias and Haven Security; some of them may have fallen, but I seriously doubted they were going to take out Elias.

Roxanne was going to be okay, but it didn't change the fact that Monty wanted to go back. If anyone was in danger, though, I felt it was us. The Darkanist with us was making me twitchy, and my gut was telling me that she was trouble.

"I have to get back," Monty said, clenching a fist. "She's in danger."

"Do you care for her?" the Darkanist said quietly. "Is she special to you?"

Monty whirled on her, tightly controlled rage in his eyes.

"Yes, she is special to me," Monty said, his voice calm with a fury I hadn't heard in a long time. "She is *very* special to me."

The Darkanist nodded while remaining looking up at him, and continued staring back.

"If you go back, Gault will reduce that building to dust along with everyone inside. *Because* she is special to you."

The words hung in the air between us as Monty continued staring at her. Peaches growled as he padded next to me. I rubbed his head as he got close. He kept rumbling, sounding like the Dark Goat on idle as he stared at the Darkanist.

*<She smells wrong.>*

*<Smells wrong how? What do you mean, boy?>*

*<She is fighting something bad. Something bad is holding her.>*

*<Something bad is holding her?>*

*<Inside. She has something bad inside.>*

*<I don't know what that means. But if you sense anything more, you stop her before whatever that bad thing is attacks us.>*

My earlier feeling of wariness ratcheted up by several levels when my hellhound informed me that the Darkanist had "something bad inside."

Outwardly, I kept my expression the same. If I drew Grim Whisper or formed Ebonsoul, I was pretty sure Monty—who was on an apocalyptic hair trigger out of his concern for Roxanne—would unleash some psycho orbs of destruction at the Darkanist.

He was usually calm and collected, but when it came to Roxanne, I wasn't going to take any chances. I could still feel the undercurrent of anger and frustration coming from his side of the room.

Peaches' prognosis wasn't as precise as I would've liked, but I trusted my hellhound's sense of smell over my sense of sight. If he said she had something bad inside—and to be fair, she *was* a Darkanist for Gault—then nothing good was going to come from having her around.

I rubbed his head again in an attempt to keep him calm. He crouched low and rumbled, keeping his slightly glowing eyes on the Darkanist. She stepped back, putting some distance between her and Peaches—not that I blamed her. I would do the same if a hellhound decided I had become a threat and started giving me major stink-eye complete with growling sound effects.

"Is something wrong with your animal?" she asked, keeping her distance. "He seems aggressive."

"He doesn't exactly do well with strangers who serve people—especially Keepers—intent on killing us," I said, without taking my eyes off her. "He's funny that way."

"What oddly specific behavior," she answered, glancing at Peaches. "Do you have many enemies who desire your death?"

"A few," I said. "With most of them, it's just a difference of beliefs."

"A difference of beliefs?"

"They believe we should be dead, and we strongly disagree."

"I can assure you, Gault is unlike any enemy you have faced," she answered, still looking at Peaches. "He won't stop until he gets what he wants. Going back to Haven would be suicide."

"Your words hold no weight here," Monty said, his voice slicing through the room in a promise of death. "You serve Gault—the same Gault who unleashed that attack on Haven.

You could just be trying to keep me, keep us, away from helping Roxanne."

I took a step forward, because Monty was sounding just this side of homicidal, but I figured it had to do with leaving Roxanne to face-off against those creatures. The Darkanist stood absolutely still, unfazed by the waves of anger and frustration coming off Monty.

She was either incredibly brave or monumentally suicidal. I was leaning toward brave since she wasn't going out of her way to antagonize Monty, or Peaches for that matter. I still didn't understand why Gault would leave her alive.

"What do I gain by keeping you from her?" the Darkanist replied. "If my goal is the end of your life, I would encourage you to go back, not warn you from returning."

She had a point.

"Your position as a Darkanist strains credulity," Monty said. "You'll excuse my doubt."

"You don't need to believe me," she continued, measuring her words, but never taking her eyes off Monty. "I can only tell you what the Keeper will do. He will find what you love, what you treasure, what you find special—and he will destroy it. That is what he does. This is what he did to me, and to anyone who serves him against their will."

"Against your will?" I asked. "He forced you to serve him?"

"Yes," she said. "Some serve him, seeking greater power. They choose to follow him willingly. For others, there is no choice."

The stare down between them lasted a few more seconds before Monty turned to the side, looking for a target for his frustration. He took a few deep breaths and composed himself.

"What is your name?" he asked. "What are you called?"

"I'm called Lotus," she said. "I know you are Tristan and

he is Simon. I am not familiar with your peculiar creature. I know he is not a normal dog."

"His name is Peaches, not creature," I said, rubbing my hellhound's enormous head. "You're right in that he's not a normal dog."

"My apologies," she said. "I meant no insult. I merely did not know his name. Peaches is a strange choice for such a fearsome-looking companion. Did you name him?"

"The name came with the companion," I said. "How can you serve Gault? He wants to destroy everything. Even if you were forced, you have to know it's the wrong move."

"I do," she said, looking at me. "I may not have much choice left, but I can choose where and how I die. By allowing myself to be captured—"

"You've passed your own death sentence," Monty said. "You know why Gault is after us. What he wants. You know what he intends to do, don't you?"

"What he wants is the First Elder Rune," Lotus said, narrowing her eyes. "The rune you...two...possess? You share the rune? How is this possible?"

"Evergreen," Monty said. "He facilitated the splitting of the rune."

"Of course," she said with a nod. "Neither of you are strong enough to divide a First Elder Rune in this way. Only a Keeper could do this so seamlessly. How did he die?"

"How did who die?" I asked.

"Evergreen?" she said. "Surely he must have expired shortly after bestowing his rune upon you two. Keepers cannot live long without their primal runes."

"Primal rune?" I asked. "What is a primal rune?"

"The rune that contains the source of the Keeper's life force and power," she explained, as if it was common knowledge. "That he shared it with the two of you is unexpected.

Neither of you are candidates for being a Keeper. It doesn't make sense."

"When we left him, he was still alive," I said, glancing at Monty. "How long can a Keeper live without their primal rune?"

"The First Keeper has limited access to several powerful runes, but to impart his primal rune as Evergreen has done? A few months, perhaps a year at most."

"He might still be alive," I said. "We need to give it back to him."

"I don't know if that's possible," she said. "Usually when a rune is imparted like this, it's at the end of a Keeper's life. However, I don't know. I've never seen a bifurcated rune like this. It's possible he possesses another source."

"How exactly can *you* see it?" I asked, glancing at Monty. "How can she see the First Elder Rune?"

"Now you know why I serve Gault," she said. "My ability to see."

"She has farsight," Monty said, narrowing his eyes at her. "Or some variation of it."

Lotus looked at Monty with surprise in her eyes.

"You know about farsight?"

"I know some of the Daughters," he said. "I didn't know Gault had conscripted some into working for him."

"I am not a Daughter," she said as Monty stared at her. "I have the ability, but I do not belong to the sect. Gault has many Arcanists with diverse gifts working for him. Some he absorbed from Verity. Others sought him out, and others—"

"He forced," Monty finished. "I would imagine those with the most powerful gifts are with him against their will."

"Most; some of the others, some of the stronger mages, serve him voluntarily," she said. "We all belong to the *Sagitta*."

"Saggy—what?" I asked. "What does that mean?"

"He used that exact term?" Monty asked, suddenly concerned. "Are you certain?"

"Yes," she said. "Sagitta is short for—"

"*Sagitta Temporis.* Arrow of Time," Monty explained. "It was an ancient group of mages who were nihilists. They believed existence was senseless and useless, that the only solution was to undo everything."

"Wonderful," I said. "We're dealing with a hardcore Nietzsche fan here?"

"If Keeper Gault belongs to *Sagitta Temporis*...they make Nietzsche look like an amateur nihilist," Monty said. "To say they were radical would be an understatement."

"They actually believed existence was senseless and useless?"

"There is only true perfection in the void of nothing," Monty said. "I believe that was their driving principle, if memory serves."

"Their driving principle sucks."

"Agreed," he replied. "It certainly explains Gault's behavior. I thought that group was wiped out centuries ago?"

"Not entirely," Lotus said. "Before he was a Keeper, Gault was one of their members and was driven into hiding by the Council of Sects. He has managed to slowly and quietly increase the number of Arrows until he could take possession of the First Elder Rune."

"Are the bulk of these Arrows also Verity Agents?"

"Yes," she answered. "They were the most impressionable. Gault used the stormblood you released at the Cloisters to convince more of Verity to join his cause. He said you were trying to disrupt the natural order of the universe and needed to be eliminated. To preserve the balance."

"So he could destroy it," Monty said. "Convenient."

"Great, another reason for Verity to be pissed at us," I

said. "Doesn't Gault have his own people? Why does he have to borrow Verity agents?"

"They are expendable to him," she said simply. "He does not care what happens to them."

"Like you?"

"No, not like her," Monty said. "*She* means something to him."

"She does?" I asked, looking at Lotus. "What do you mean to Gault?"

"I really need some tea," Monty said, moving to the kitchen. "How does Gault track you?"

"Track her?" I asked. "Why would he—?"

"She's valuable to him," Monty finished, looking at Lotus. "That group back at Haven, it wasn't just for Ramirez, Roxanne, or us. That was the deflection. Wasn't it?"

Lotus looked down at the floor.

"Partially. They were tasked with bringing me back," she said, her voice low. "Their mission was to kill you and recapture me."

The air around our space suddenly became charged with energy. Monty stared at Lotus from the kitchen as several violet-and-black energy orbs floated around his body. I hadn't even seen a finger-wiggle. Monty was getting scary good at forming these orbs of destruction without warning.

"Whoa, Monty, what are you doing?" I asked, looking around. "We're not under attack."

"Don't be so sure," he said, still staring at Lotus. "If I wanted to get near an enemy, the easiest way would be to leave behind a willing hostage, someone I could then use to attack from the inside, when they were vulnerable or distracted." He pointed at Lotus. "Someone like her."

I had to admit it was a good idea, and it gave me pause.

"Is that what you are?" I asked. "Some kind of Trojan horse? Get close and then attack us when we least expect it?"

Lotus raised her cuffed wrists.

"It would be somewhat difficult to mount any type of attack wearing these," she said. "All of my abilities, including most of my sight, have been neutralized."

"But you *were* able to see the First Elder Rune," I said. "How?"

"It's the First Elder Rune," she said matter-of-factly as she shrugged. "Whoever hid it was quite skilled, but that rune is almost impossible to hide from someone like me, someone with my ability—even with these inhibitor cuffs on. Keeper Evergreen would have known this."

"Why should we let you live?" Monty asked, still doing his scary mage impression. The orbs floating around him crackled with power as he looked at her. "You are an obvious liability, one that will only lead Gault to us. From what I've learned about Gault, killing you would be a mercy, compared to what he would do to you."

I stared at Monty.

"We're not going to kill her," I said. "Isn't that against the mage Geneva Conventions or something?"

"No such conventions exist," Monty said, his voice hard, before turning to Lotus. "You didn't answer my question."

"You're right," she said. "Killing me would remove an obvious liability. But it wouldn't stop Gault, only delay his plan."

She pulled down on the collar of her shirt and revealed a circle of symbols tattooed into her skin just under her collarbone. The symbols were written in runes I couldn't understand, but judging from how Monty's face paled at the sight of them, I knew they were bad.

In the center of the circle of runes, I saw a group of eight arrows all pointing outward from a common center. They pointed to eight specific symbols within the circle, which were colored in red.

"What?" I asked, looking from Monty to Lotus. "What is that?"

"A death cast," Monty said as he absorbed his orbs. "If we kill her, it would unleash an entropic dissolution—"

"Fed by my life force," Lotus finished. "It was how he forced us to serve."

"How strong?" Monty asked, his voice low. "How strong a dissolution?"

"Not very," Lotus said. "Probably powerful enough to engulf this entire building with everyone inside."

"The entire building?" I said. "Olga would lose her mind if we dissolved the Moscow."

"To say the least," Monty added, examining the runes. "It's triggered upon your death?"

"Yes," Lotus said. "Immediately upon my demise."

"You're a walking time bomb," I said, taking a few steps back from her. "Can he activate that thing remotely?"

"No," she said, shaking her head. "It requires death, a spoken command, or that he touch the symbol to activate it. He calls it his insurance policy. Many of the Dark Arcanists carry a similar symbol."

"I have a feeling yours is unique and more potent," Monty said as she covered the symbol again. "The circle of runes around it, do you know what it means?"

"No," she said. "He said it was to keep me safe from the power of the symbol."

"He lied," Monty said, but revealed nothing further. "We can't stay here much longer. If Gault has a way of finding you, he will locate you here eventually. We need to get to a deadzone."

"What kind of dead zone?" I asked. "Like a neutral zone?"

"No, we need a space devoid of an energy signature," he said. "A void location."

"Which is where, exactly?"

"Right now, we can use my uncle's room," Monty said, looking back at our space. "It will serve our purposes, at least temporarily."

"What if she gets lost in there?" I asked. "You know Dex has modified that space."

"It can't be helped," he said. "If she remains out in the open, Gault will find and eliminate her."

"Not good," I said, glancing at Lotus. "What about her cuffs?"

"They need to stay on," he answered. "I would imagine the only thing keeping her hidden at the moment are those cuffs."

"We can't send her into that room alone," I said. "Do you have any way of controlling where it leads?"

"No, that would solely be under my uncle's control," he said. "But I may have a solution."

"Excellent. Is it a solution that doesn't involve disintegrating or exploding the building?" I asked. "A non-destructive method would be nice for a change."

"Most of my methods are non-destructive," he said. "I can create a temporary interstice."

"That sounds excellent. What is it?"

"A pocket dimension where that symbol can be hidden for the time being," he said. "The runes around that symbol contain an immense amount of power. Even with our defenses here, there's no guarantee he hasn't found us already."

A knock at the door caused my heart to skip several beats.

# ELEVEN

I just barely managed to keep my heart inside my chest as Monty motioned for me to open the door.

"I'm not in the mood to dance with ogres right now. Who is it?" I asked Monty as I headed to the door.

Monty closed his eyes for half a second before answering.

"Olga," Monty said, moving Lotus to the conference room. "Entertain her while I create the space for our guest away from curious eyes."

"Why would you need to move her from—oh, that makes sense," I said when he pointed at the cuffs. "That would probably give Olga the wrong impression."

"Agreed," Monty said, motioning to the conference room and leading Lotus away. "Keep her occupied for a few minutes while I relocate our guest."

"About your last conversation with Olga—"

"Use your diplomacy," Monty called out as he walked away. "I'm sure you won't do anything to anger her in the brief moment you're alone with her."

"Right," I muttered to myself as I reached the door. "Keep things cool."

It always amazed me how Olga knew when we were home. I wondered if she had some kind of detection system that let her know we were in the building.

I opened the door and she peered imperially down at me with her icy blue eyes, as if she were doing me a favor by allowing me to breathe the same air as her.

She wore a lightly runed black Chanel pantsuit with a matching pair of black Chanel heels. Her hair was pulled back in a severe bun that accentuated her scowl as she gazed down her nose at me.

"Stronk," she said, her accent extra thick. "Good, you are home."

I stepped back, making room for her and her oversized sense of importance, allowing her full access to the space.

"Hello, Olga," I said, glancing at my vigilant hellhound. "Good morning."

"It is *not* good morning," she corrected. "Where is *prepodavatel*, Cecelia's teacher?"

"He's in the back," I said. "He'll be right out. Can I get you something to drink? Coffee?"

"No coffee," she said, approaching my hellhound who remained vigilant. "*Persiki* is being good dog, yes?"

She tapped Peaches on the head lightly and he graciously allowed her to keep her fingers. He gave me a look and chuffed before padding away to the conference area.

"He's always a good dog," I answered, following him with my gaze. "How are you? Is the building okay?"

Olga made her way over to one of the lounges, avoiding the Hansen—everyone except Cece avoided the Hansen. She sat down, crossed one leg over the other, rested her hands on her knees, and stared at me.

Fine, I was horrible at small talk. Olga and I had nothing in common aside from the fact that, according to Monty, she was some sort of Ice Queen royalty with the potential to be an insanely strong ice mage, and I enjoyed drinking ice water when I wasn't savoring my amazing javambrosia.

I was coming to the conclusion that she didn't like me much, and I certainly wasn't a fan of the glare-and-scowl club she was clearly the president of, her being an expert in holding an expression of minimal tolerance whenever we interacted.

Specks of dust probably felt more warmth from her than what she demonstrated to me when she spoke in my direction. It was never a conversation between us, more like an interrogation where I was given the privilege of responding whenever she deemed I was worthy.

I felt a surge of energy and imagined that Monty had created his intersection space for Lotus. It disappeared almost as soon as I sensed it. I really hoped Gault hadn't tracked Lotus to our location; if he had, I had a feeling that the Moscow, like Haven, was about to undergo major renovations.

"Building is good. No more holes. That is good."

Monty appeared from the back just as the conversation turned to building renovations. I let out a sigh of relief and made to leave when Olga let out a sharp cough. For a split second, I was back in sixth grade as Mrs. Fenster called me to the board to work out a math problem I had no clue how to complete.

"Stay, Stronk. We must talk."

I froze in place and slowly backtracked into the reception area.

"What would you like to talk about?" I asked as I made myself comfortable, avoiding the Hansen. Roxanne may have been busy dealing with angry creatures, but I was sure she would sense if we sat on it, and would unleash the appropriate wrath when she had a moment. "Is something on your mind?"

"Cecelia," Monty said. "She would like to discuss Cecelia's magical education."

"Yes," Olga said with a nod. "This is very important. Cecelia too strong to live here. I have ice everywhere, then water everywhere." She waved an arm around. "Guardian dog is too big and eats like horse. She needs more space, but cannot go home. Too dangerous at home."

"Too dangerous?" I asked. "Why would it be too dangerous?"

"Cecelia is special," Olga said, looking away. "If she go home, they will attack. It will be bad for her, for Jotnar, and for my people. She cannot go home."

"I guess she can stay here with us," I said. "But we are hardly ever here."

"Too dangerous to stay with you. She break building because of you, Stronk," she said, narrowing her eyes at me. "Cecelia say *you* help her break my building."

I opened my mouth to respond and closed it again.

I was about to protest, but thought better of it. Some battles were better off left unfought—this was one of them. Besides, I would have given me up, too, if I were Cece.

Cece never stood a chance under that gaze of disapproval mixed with contempt, which only displeased parents or elderly relatives could pull off with a practiced ease. For Olga, disapproval with a large dose of contempt was the resting expression on her face.

"What do you propose?" Monty said. "I'm open to your suggestions."

"This is good," Olga said with a nod. "Cecelia will go to your uncle school. There she will be safe."

I couldn't disagree.

Dexter's School of Battle Magic was probably the safest location for Cece on this or any plane. It just surprised me that this would be her suggestion.

"Are you certain?" Monty asked. "She would be off-plane."

"I am not good aunt," she said. "Cecelia needs more... contact. I am busy, always away. Your uncle is good person and can help her."

"He can," Monty said. "Her exposure to danger would also be greatly reduced. A move there would increase her overall safety."

"Yes, that is safe. Cecelia is lonely. She is little girl with no friends here. In your uncle school, she has friend...Peanut?"

Monty nodded.

"They are close in age and Peanut is a good influence on Cecelia," Monty said. "I can assume you have discussed this with my uncle?"

"Yes, you stay her main teacher, your uncle helps her when you are busy," Olga answered, satisfied with her solution. "You must get her ready for Jotnar trials, and your uncle is very powerful. He will also help. This is good."

"I'm sure I can come to some arrangement with my uncle regarding Cecelia's instruction," Monty said. "Are you sure you want me to remain her main instructor? My uncle is much more qualified than I."

"Cecelia wants you," Olga said, pointing at Monty. "You stay as main teacher. Yes?"

"If that is her request, then I will honor it, of course," Monty said with a short bow. "How soon is Cecelia moving to the school?"

"One week," Olga said. "Must finish details with her family, then she goes."

"Well," I said. "Sounds like you don't need me for any of this. I'm glad Cece will be at the school. She will definitely be in good hands. You made the right decision."

I made to leave the reception area and Olga cleared her throat again.

"Wait," she said. It wasn't a request but more along the lines of a command. "I will speak with you, Stronk."

"Sure," I said. "How can I help you?"

"Not me, Cecelia," Olga said, glancing at Monty—and for the first time ever, she looked uncomfortable. "Cecelia says you help her. Different from main teacher. She wants you to keep helping."

"Help her?" I said, confused. "How do I help her?"

"You are different than main teacher," she said. "He is as he should be, hard, like hammer. You...you are soft, like pillow."

I caught Monty looking away and hiding a smile, before a sudden series of convenient coughs forced him to cover his face.

"I'm soft...like a pillow?" I repeated, certain that something was lost in translation. "She wants me to keep helping because I'm soft like a pillow?"

"Good, you understand," Olga said with a nod. "He is like hammer." She pointed at Monty. "And you are like pillow. You work together." She clasped her hands together in a loud clap. "You make Cecelia strongest Jotnar."

I thought back to everything Cece had done up to this point.

"I would say she's pretty strong already," I answered, still mildly insulted that I was *soft, like pillow.* "How am I supposed to help her get stronger?"

"Not you alone, together," Olga clarified, her voice grim. "She *must* pass trials. Life or death. Do you understand? Fail means die. If Cecelia dies, her family will be angry. Very angry. They will challenge and look for blood revenge."

"Blood revenge?"

"Blood vengeance," Monty explained. "Not a situation we want to experience."

"No, you do not want," Olga said with a shake of her head.

"This is very bad. You train Cecelia, she pass trials, no blood revenge."

I understood the threat of menace in Olga's voice. Whatever Cece was going to become, it seemed most of it depended on her passing these trials. I didn't look forward to facing whatever this blood vengeance was. I had enough situations dealing with blood to last me several lifetimes. Adding another wasn't on my to-do list.

"We understand," Monty said as I nodded silently. "She will pass her trials."

She reached into her jacket and pulled out a small, silver card, and handed it to Monty. A dark expression crossed her face as she looked at the card.

"This is message for you," she said, pointing at the card. "From cousin."

"From my cousin?" Monty asked, examining the card. "Did this cousin have a name?"

"He ask for you," she said, still looking at the card. "No give me name, just your cousin. He ask for Tristan Montague. He knows you."

"It would appear so," Monty said. "Did he say anything else?"

"He give me this card for you," she continued. "He is waiting, he said. This man was not honest. His mouth speaks peace, but his eyes hold death. Do not trust this *cousin*. Can you read message?"

Monty nodded as he looked at the card. A subtle wave of rage crossed Monty's face as he read the card. He flexed his jaw for several seconds before he passed the card to me.

"Thank you for passing along the message and your concern," Monty said. "I will see to it that the family matter with my *cousin* is dealt with."

"Good. Not in building," Olga warned. "Do *not* break building."

"I can assure you no damage will come to the building."

Olga stood and headed to the door, pausing at the threshold.

"Make sure no damage comes to you. This cousin has eyes of killer."

She left the space. I looked down at the card and saw it was written in runes, which I couldn't make out.

"Monty?" I said, holding up the card. "My rune reading is a little rusty. What does this say?"

He gestured and the card shimmered with a silver glint.

"You can read it now," Monty said.

On one side, it read:

*To the Montague & Strong Detective Agency*

On the opposite side, it read:

*Tristan,*

*You have something of great value to me.*

*I would prefer to have it returned to me without bloodshed, but as you have witnessed, I'm not averse to spilling blood to attain my objectives.*

*Your landlady was a gracious hostess. She assured me that you will get this message with the utmost urgency.*

*Let's discuss the terms of your exchange at the nearby neutral zone —James informs me he is a good friend, and has extended every courtesy to me while I await you and Strong.*

*Do not tarry.*

*G.*

"That bastard," I said and read the card again. "He's bragging about being here."

Monty nodded.

"He's letting us know he can reach us," Monty said. "He attacked Ramirez and the NYTF, unleashed his minions in Haven, paid Olga a visit here, and is currently sitting—"

"In the Randy Rump," I finished. "Is Jimmy in danger?"

"I don't think so," he said, heading to the room where

Ramirez slept. "He mentioned he was in a neutral zone, which means he knows the repercussions for violence while there."

"It was a subtle, not-so-subtle threat," I said. "He's willing to kill to get what he wants."

"Yes, he's willing to employ lethal measures," Monty said as he gestured and formed a green circle under Ramirez. "He's willing to throw lives away for his cause. Whether he's willing to take lives personally is another matter entirely."

"We're going to find out, aren't we?"

"Right after we send Ramirez someplace safe, yes," Monty said as the circle began to glow brighter. "It's been my experience that cowards enjoy calling for war and death, but rarely take up arms themselves, comfortable in the fact that others will do the dying for them."

"Where are you sending Angel? Same place as Lotus?"

"No," Monty said. "Lotus is in an interstice designed to nullify her energy signature and the entropic symbol in her skin. Ramirez will be going to my uncle for the time being. He'll be able to recover safely there."

"That school is going to get crowded," I said. "Entropic symbol? Is that what that arrow tattoo means?"

"The arrows are a symbol for entropy," he said as Ramirez disappeared. "It's the circle of runes around it that concern me. Those were proto-runes—think of them as a runic beacon of sorts."

"A locator?" I asked. "That symbol tells Gault where she is?"

"I think it's more than that," he said as we left the small room. "From what I could determine, Lotus is an extension of Gault—she is connected to him somehow."

"What?"

"It's not just her eyes that make her special to him," he

said. "He needs her to complete the transference of the First Elder Rune. She is a receptacle of sorts."

"He can't just rip the rune out of us?"

"I don't think it's that easy, but I'm sure he will try."

"Now I feel all reassured," I said as we headed to the door. "And we're going to go have a chat with him—without an army of mages, I'm guessing?"

"You guess correctly," Monty said. "Call your hound while I reset the failsafes."

He started touching several parts of the door in sequence.

*<Let's go, boy. We're going to go see Jimmy.>*

Peaches blinked in next to me a second later.

*<He has good meat. Can I get meat from the bear man?>*

*<I'm sure he'll give you some as soon as we get there. Someone else is going to be there. though—someone bad. Do not attack unless I say so. Got it?>*

*<Get meat from the bear man, attack the bad person if he tries to hurt you.>*

*<Close enough. Let's go.>*

Monty finished setting up the failsafes and we headed out of the Moscow.

# TWELVE

The area around the Randy Rump was deserted.

Mid-morning in the up-and-coming Chelsea area was usually buzzing with activity. The Randy Rump would be serving the normal clientele on its way to and from work.

It was never crowded during the day with traffic being brisk, but I saw no one entering or leaving the restaurant-bar.

Odd, but not necessarily surprising.

The lunch crowd was due to arrive in about an hour or so, in addition to the regulars who used the Rump as an unofficial work space. Jimmy never asked anyone to leave. He felt that having people there at all hours of the day was good for business and helped promote the Rump as a neutral space.

To look down the street and see it empty was strange, and twisted my stomach into a tight knot. There was something off with the image. On a deep level my brain knew and protested the wrongness I saw. It looked staged—and that's when I realized that, in a very real way, it was.

Gault had probably made it so that he could meet us alone, or at the very least with only his own people in the area around us. The emptiness was a subtle display of his power and influence.

I didn't like it.

Everything in my body and brain was screaming at me to turn around and run the other way, putting as much distance as possible between me and the Rump. I clamped down on the primitive desire for flight as we walked down the empty street.

"These streets are usually packed with people," I said, looking around. "You think he—?"

"Most likely," Monty said. "They may seem empty, but we are surrounded by what you like to call Darkanists. Look for yourself."

I briefly closed my eyes, expanding my senses outward as we approached the Randy Rump. At first I didn't feel anything; and then suddenly as if a curtain had been lifted, I felt them all around us.

None of the Darkanists were on or in the Randy Rump, but every street around us was filled with them. The roofs of the buildings opposite the Rump were populated by them.

I sensed no overt energy signatures, but it was closer to sensing pockets of nothingness all around us. It was as if I could feel the opposite of energy signatures. The presence was too scattered for me to get a count of how many were around us, but I knew it was substantial.

We were surrounded by a small army of fairly powerful mages.

"How is he keeping everyone else away?" I asked, looking around. "He doesn't have the place locked down, does he?"

"Aversion runes and the Darkanists I would imagine."

"They don't read like the usual energy signatures."

"He's using a powerful masking ability," Monty said as we crossed the street. "I doubt we could even sense them if we didn't possess the First Elder Rune."

I nodded but remained silent.

Several of the Darkanists shifted positions as we reached the entrance to the Rump. They were close enough to launch an attack, but just out of reach for my senses to pinpoint accurate numbers.

"I'm not sensing any of the creature squad, are you?"

"Ogres, trollgres, and thralls would probably prove too unwieldy to mask and control—especially the thralls, I think," he said as we paused at the door. "If they are close, he won't reveal them just yet. Remember, we're here to negotiate an exchange."

"That's what I'm concerned about," I said. "An exchange of what? I know what he wants from us. He doesn't have anything I want. Do you want anything from him?"

"Nothing that comes to mind, no."

"Then this whole *exchange* sounds like an excuse to get us here, into this trap, where he wants us."

"Not much of a choice there," Monty said. "Better for us to meet here than to have him enact another assault, like on Haven."

"Do you think he's going to honor the Rump's neutral status?"

"Not in the slightest," Monty said, dusting off a sleeve. "We will be civil until it's time to be rude. He's a Keeper and presents a significant threat."

"Which means you want me to use diplomacy?"

He slowly shook his head.

"Our previous attempts at diplomacy and tact have been less than stellar," he said. "Let's hear what he has to say and act accordingly. It's possible he's here to reason with us."

I gave him a *you can't be serious* stare.

"It's also possible he's here to shred us to pieces," I said, looking around the area around the Rump. "I really doubt all these Darkanists are here to convince us to reason with the Keeper."

"True," Monty said, glancing around. "Keep your wits about you, and your weapons handy. We may need them."

I nodded as Monty pushed the door and we stepped into the Randy Rump. The Rump was mostly empty during the day—being a neutral zone for the magical community meant it kept night hours most of the time.

Even though it serviced normals, the majority of the patrons were night owls, arriving usually around sundown.

Jimmy stood behind the counter, wearing his usual white shirt and apron. He bent behind the counter and produced a large titanium bowl of pastrami for my hellhound before glancing over to the corner.

I nudged my hound over to the bowl and followed Jimmy's gaze with my own. Sitting at one of the corner tables, I noticed an older man.

*<Eat the meat, but stay alert, boy.>*

*<That man over there smells bad, like the other woman.>*

*<Keep your eyes open. If he starts to attack, stop him.>*

*<Can I remove his arm?>*

*<He's dangerous and powerful. Let me and Monty speak to him first.>*

*<He smells strong, but not stronger than the old bird man and his woman.>*

*<He could be hiding his strength right now.>*

*<If he tries to hurt you, then I will remove his arm.>*

*<If he attacks, we'll stop him, but I want you to be careful. There's something off about this whole thing.>*

*<I'll be careful, after I eat the meat.>*

The older man sat at one of the larger tables and took a long pull from his mug of coffee as he looked out of the window into the street. I glanced at Jimmy and motioned for my usual.

Jimmy nodded and began preparing our drinks.

The man appeared normal. If this was the Keeper, he was seriously underwhelming. I barely sensed an energy signature outside of the normal. There was no presence of earth-shattering power, or at least not that I could sense.

If I went by appearances, this was a gentleman enjoying a morning cup of coffee—surrounded by Darkanists and sitting in an eerily empty restaurant-bar.

Two empty chairs sat opposite the older man. He looked in our direction, fixing us with his gaze before giving us a small smile and motioning to the two chairs in front of him with his mug. His black hair was cut short on the sides—not quite a screaming eagle, but neat. His piercing gray eyes took us in as we crossed the floor.

He wore an impeccable, runed black Zegna suit, one that gave Monty a run for his money. It was offset by a pale gray Tom Ford shirt, accented with a black Turnbull & Asser tie, and finished off by a pair of black Hermes shoes.

It was the typical mageiform, but at the highest level of quality. The subtle runes in his suit shimmered with power, and his energy signature continued to feel almost non-existent as he sat there waiting for us.

The lack of a substantial energy signature should have clued me in to what kind of threat we were facing.

Monty and I approached his table and sat.

"Thank you for coming," Gault said, his voice a rich tenor. He took another pull from his cup. "I expected no less from the both of you."

My hellhound had inhaled the meat in record time and padded over to where I sat. He sat back on his haunches and released a low rumble, which ended in a menacing growl as he focused on Gault.

"A hellhound," Gault continued as he looked at me, then at Peaches without a trace of fear. "You're bonded. I'm impressed. Especially considering your lack of, how would I put it...presence? Forgive me, but you don't present much of a threat, even with a hellhound bondmate."

Peaches released another low growl and I almost joined him.

"It would be a mistake to judge someone by their appearance," I said. "I mean, you look like a decrepit, simpleminded, senior citizen, but you don't hear me calling you any names, no matter how accurate they may be."

Anger flitted across his eyes as he kept his gaze on me. He may have been powerful, but he was still a mage—which meant he had buttons the size of basketballs just waiting for me to push.

Jimmy came by and brought my mug of coffee, and then slid a large cup of Earl Grey in front of Monty, who nodded his thanks.

"James," Gault said, "I would appreciate it if would you close your establishment. I have some delicate business matters to discuss with these gentlemen."

"I don't feel comfortable leaving—" Jimmy began before Gault raised a hand.

"Rest assured, no damage will come to your place of business," Gault reassured him with a soothing voice. "I have no wish to incur the wrath of the Dark Council by destroying one of their neutral zones. The Randy Rump will remain unscathed should any violence occur, though I don't anticipate any. You have my word."

I thought about the damage at Haven. I trusted his word about as much as I trusted my hellhound to refuse a fresh sausage.

Jimmy looked at Monty and me, made up his mind, and then nodded.

"Go ahead, Jimmy," I said, glancing at him. "We won't let anything happen inside. The Rump is safe."

"I'm going to hold you to that," he said. "Keep this place safe."

"As safe as my own home."

Jimmy frowned before nodding and heading off to the back room. It could be he heard about the recent hole Cece punched into the Moscow—which wasn't entirely my fault, so it didn't count.

"It's not every day you see a werebear in this city," Gault said, looking after Jimmy as he walked away. "And running a neutral zone at that."

"James is very good at maintaining the neutrality of this location," Monty said, "despite the violence that has occurred here in the past."

"Violence that you two were directly responsible for," Gault said. "At least it seems that way from my understanding. Extenuating circumstances?"

"You could say that," Monty replied. "Overzealous and deluded mages have a tendency to react poorly when faced with direct opposition. Something I'm sure you have experience with."

Gault's expression darkened for a brief moment before the small smile returned. I removed the silver card with the message from a pocket and placed it on the table between us.

I took the opportunity to take a long pull of Deathwish and basked in the aroma of the javambrosia filling my lungs as the robust flavor caressed my tastebuds.

Moments later, I felt the failsafes around the Rump fall into place as Jimmy sealed the Randy Rump. He must have left through one of the other exits, because he didn't return to the area where we sat.

"You wanted to see us," I said, pointing at the card. "We're here."

Gault leaned back and looked out the window again.

"You would be surprised how often a simple invitation

results in an escalation of violence," he said, gazing out into the street. "I remember this area when it was a small port just coming into its own. This country was in its infancy then, barely aware of its potential and power. Much like you two."

I didn't appreciate being compared to an infant, but I managed to let the insult pass.

I wasn't in a hurry to see how dangerous Gault was. If we could somehow manage to have a non-magical conversation, I was all for it. Did I think it could actually happen? Not in a million years.

"We have no desire to escalate this into a violent confrontation," Monty said, after sipping some of his tea. "What do you want?"

"Everything and nothing," Gault said, turning to look at Monty. "Let's start with the tangible. You apprehended one of my people—a Dark Arcanist."

"What?" Monty said as I kept my expression impassive. "We've faced many Dark Arcanists. You expect us to remember every one we have encountered?"

It looked like she was more important than I originally thought, especially if Gault was asking for her. I made a mental note, but remained silent.

Gault smiled and took another pull from his mug before staring at Monty again. He placed the mug gently on the table between us without making a sound, then slowly rotated it while he kept his gaze fixed on the street outside.

"I understand that you feel you must do this," he said. "That through some misguided sense of righteousness, you feel you must stand in my way. I would advise you to change course—now, while you still can. You cannot stop me. At most, you will be an irksome and insignificant delay, but you will *not* stop me."

As a mage it meant his ego was as strong as an eggshell and as large as a planet.

I went to work.

"Stop you from what?" I asked. "What do you think we want to stop you from doing?"

He turned to me as if seeing me for the first time, a mild look of contempt crossing his features. I had managed to annoy him, but I was just getting started.

"I don't need to explain myself to you," he said, narrowing his eyes at me. "I don't need to explain myself to anyone."

"Is that because you're clueless?"

He gave me a hard stare and I could sense his anger rising.

"Has anyone ever told you that your words could get you killed?"

"It's been mentioned once or twice."

"Yet you lack the wisdom to heed the warnings?"

"I don't lack the wisdom," I said. "I'm just not in awe of the power you may wield."

"Because you have no comprehension of the power that lies before you," Gault said. "If you had an inkling of the power I control—"

"I would still be unimpressed," I finished. "Power is meaningless if all you do is bully people with it. Seems to me that people with power have a tendency to abuse that power. They expect others to bow down to them just because they're stronger."

"The strong will always subjugate the weak," he said. "It is the natural order of things."

"Bullshit," I said, keeping tight control of the anger that was rising inside of me. "That's the excuse deluded tyrants use to justify their actions. The strong only subjugate the weak when no one dares to stop them."

"And you dare?"

"I do," I said. "There's always someone stronger, and everyone has a weakness of some kind."

"I have no such weaknesses," he said with a tight smile.

"You sit before someone who could end your existence with a mere gesture. Do you seek death?"

I took a long pull from my coffee.

Part of it was because I really needed coffee, but more importantly, I needed to buy myself a few seconds to gather my thoughts and stomp on the fear that was wrapping itself around me and squeezing the air out of my throat.

"For someone without any weaknesses, you sure are making a strong case to have this Lotus returned to you," I said. "Why do you need this Darkanist if you are an all-powerful Keeper? Can't you just snap your all-powerful fingers and make her appear?"

"I never mentioned a gender," he said quietly. "You know where she is."

"I don't, and even if I did, I wouldn't share that information with you."

"Your insolence will cut your life short," Gault said with a low growl.

"Heard that one, too," I said. "Maybe you aren't as powerful as you would like us to believe?"

"I am a Keeper," he said and flexed his energy signature. "You doubt my power?"

"In my experience, I've found that those who need to explain how powerful they are usually aren't very powerful at all," I answered, keeping my words even and measured as his energy signature began filling the Randy Rump. "It's usually all bark and no bite. The weaker they are, the louder the bark."

I gripped the edge of the table to keep my hands from shaking. His energy signature felt like someone was slowly placing an enormous weight on my shoulders. I was beginning to feel compressed as I sat at the table and looked up to make sure the ceiling wasn't actually pressing down on me.

"That is merely a small sampling of my power," he said. "I doubt you could withstand more."

I doubted I could withstand more either, but I wasn't going to let him know that. Beside me, I could feel my hell-hound fighting against the presence of this energy signature, and even Monty was flexing his jaw as he dealt with the waves of energy flowing around us.

"You have something that belongs to me," he said. "Return it and I will let you live out the rest of your days, however short, in relative peace. Disobey me, and your end will be long and torturous. You will find, in the end, that you *will* comply."

"What exactly do you want?"

"The Lotus," he said, his voice a promise of pain. "You hid it from me. Reveal its location and I promise to only make you suffer for days before ending your lives. Refuse me and I will keep you alive until you beg for death."

His answer threw me, because he had used her name as a title and called her an "it." I'd fully expected him to say the First Elder Rune. His saying the Lotus confused me. It must have shown on my face because he took another pull from his mug and smiled at me.

"You expected me to say the First Elder Rune, yes?"

"Yes," I said. "I did, actually."

"You are both so out of your depth, you have no idea where the bottom is," he said. "I *know* you have the rune. I can sense it as easily as I can sense this table under my hand. I knew the moment that fool, Evergreen, gave it to you. He made a fatal error. Giving the First Elder Rune to you only makes my task easier."

"You need this Lotus for something else," Monty said. "Something beyond the transference."

"Full marks for intelligence, mage," Gault said. "The First Elder Rune is only the beginning of the end. There is more, so much more. Your limited imaginations couldn't comprehend the machinations I have set in motion. I will usher in a new age of magic."

"A new age?" I said. "You want to destroy—"

"You think I want to destroy everything?" he asked. "That I want to see it all burn?"

"Well, yes," I said. "Something like that."

"Myopic fools," he said, looking outside again. "They only told you enough to get you killed. Even Evergreen was short-sighted, and he was the most forward-thinking of them. He scoffed and rebuked me when I explained my vision of a new world to him. I will restore balance and usher in a new golden age."

"By destroying everything," Monty said. "You will undo reality."

"To recreate it," Gault explained. "I can reestablish the necessary balance in this world. Magic could be a common thing. Everyone and anyone could learn to manipulate energy."

"Everyone could learn?" I asked. "You want *everyone* to have access to magic? You think that would be a *good* idea?"

"The rune you hold is forbidden to most mages, Catalyst," Gault said. "Do you know what that causes?"

"Safety?" I said. "You keep the rune out of the wrong hands?"

"Envy, strife, animosity," Gault said. "It causes mages to covet that which they can't have. It breeds contempt and hatred. It starts wars."

"And your solution is to give everyone the power?" I asked in disbelief. "That's your idea of peace?"

"My world would be egalitarian, not one of elites, of sects hidden away hoarding and wielding power, while the masses are dominated and controlled. Everyone would be equal."

"Except some would be more equal than others, right?" I

asked. "I mean some would have more power before everyone is equal, right?"

"Of course, in the beginning, instruction would be needed," he said, revealing what I already knew. "There will be those that need to be guided in the new ways of the world."

"With you and your chosen doing all of the guiding and showing?"

"I will be the most equipped to do so, at least at first, yes," he said. "It is the only way."

"Wow, that sounds like a magical utopia," I said, letting the anger lace my words. "And all it takes is the destruction of everything? Sounds easy enough."

"You could never comprehend my plan," he said, shaking his head. "Even now in your ignorance, you resort to mockery, when I offer the world, peace, and yes, a real magical utopia."

"I do mock you," I said, keeping my voice low. "For all that power you claim to have, it looks like you can't usher in your new age without oh, I don't know, destroying everything first. Sounds like a megalomaniac with a side of delusions of grandeur and a sprinkling of generous amounts of genocide."

"I am no such thing. I am a visionary. Don't you understand that the path we are on will only lead to another inevitable war?"

"Why? Because you say so?"

"Because I have lived through them," he said, his voice bitter. "I have seen the pattern repeat itself countless times. I have the means to interrupt the cycle. You can be part of the solution, rather than an obstacle."

"Interrupt the cycle? By unleashing entropy," Monty said. "The annihilation of everything."

"What is the cost of the billions on this plane weighed against the cost of trillions across several planes?" Gault asked. "The needs of the many will always outweigh the needs of the few, or the one."

"Unless you're one of the few, or the one."

"You are a battlemage, Montague," he said, looking at Monty. "You know my words are true. You have lived through the horrors of war. I have seen it repeated over and over. You have an opportunity here to prevent the next war. To prevent war from ever visiting this plane again."

"By obliterating every life that currently exists?" Monty asked. "That is not a solution, that is madness."

"You're just like the others, short-sighted and fearful," Gault answered as anger laced his words. "People like you fear change, fear the unknown. Your kind cannot be ushered peacefully into a new age, you must be forced, kicking and screaming with the clenched fist of violence."

"If that was your sales pitch, it was an epic fail," I said. "With all due respect to your visionary status, your plan sucks."

"You would never understand," he said, narrowing his eyes at me as more energy flowed from him. "How could you? You have the understanding of children who are staring into the infinite. You cannot possibly comprehend what I intend to do. What I *will* do."

"I'd really like to hear about this grand plan, but it all falls apart for me at the kill everyone part," I said. "Maybe if you explain *that* aspect of your non-megalomaniacal vision again?"

"No. You've only come here because you know I threaten everything and everyone you hold dear," he said with a short sigh. "There is no room for learning within your minds. You are merely tools to be used and then discarded, like the rest. Enough conversation—give me the Lotus, or die."

# THIRTEEN

"No," Monty said as we backed away from the table. "She is not your property or a tool to be used and discarded."

"You are wrong on both counts," Gault said. "I created her, and she has only one purpose: to die for me. Like you, runebearer, she must fulfill her purpose."

"I'm going to have to second what Monty said," I answered, drawing Grim Whisper. "She's not yours and she's not a tool to be used."

"Very well," Gault said. "We shall do this in a way you understand...with blood and pain."

Peaches let out a low rumble as Gault placed his mug down slowly on the table. Energy flowed around him as he stared at us.

"What happened to not destroying the Randy Rump?"

"I lied."

He slashed a hand in front of him and blasted us with a wave of energy.

Monty threw up a shield to deflect most of the impact as I fired at Gault. The wave of energy punched into us and flung Monty across the floor into the glass facade making up the front of the Rump, while it smacked me into a nearby wall...hard.

Gault stood with a look of mild surprise on his face as we bounced off the hard surfaces and got back to our feet.

"You're still alive?" he said. "I'm impressed. I will strive to inflict greater pain on you both, then."

I didn't understand what he meant until I glanced behind Monty. The entire facade of the Randy Rump facing the street had exploded into small particles behind Monty.

"Holy hell," I muttered under my breath as the wall I crashed into disintegrated. "What the—?"

I dove forward as another wave of energy headed my way. I fired Grim Whisper as I rolled into a crouch, but my entropy rounds didn't even reach him. I saw Peaches blink out and reappear on a collision course for Gault.

Gault stood still and waited for my hellhound.

"Quaint, but ineffective," Gault said as he caught Peaches by the scruff, gestured with his opposite hand, and tossed him outside, through a rune-inscribed window, shattering it using my hellhound's body. "That should slow him down."

Peaches landed across the street, bounced for several feet and came to a stop as he crashed into a brick wall, cratering it. He shook himself off, took several steps toward the Rump and collapsed with a whine.

"What did you do to my hellhound?" I demanded as I formed Ebonsoul. "What did you do?"

"I merely removed a layer of indestructibility," Gault said, forming a pair of bright blue orbs and releasing them. "If I were you, I'd be more concerned with your own imminent demise. I'll end your infernal creature after I rip the First Elder Rune from your bodies."

<Run, boy! He's too strong and he made you weak. You need to run away! Get safe!>

<Wherever you go, I go.>

Peaches managed to get to his feet and blink out, only to reappear next to me a moment later.

*<I don't want to lose you. You can get away.>*

*<You can't lose me. I'm your bondmate.>*

"Touching," Gault said. "Give me the Lotus, and I may be persuaded to spare the hellhound. Deny me, and I will make sure you watch while I rip his heart out from his chest."

"Fuck you," I said. "Peaches, run, now!"

"Futile," Gault said as he walked in my direction. He gestured and trapped Peaches in a light blue lattice, forcing him flat to the ground. Peaches growled and tried to stand, but he was rooted to one spot. "You are the catalyst; therefore you have the privilege of dying first. With you dead, this will be much easier." He glanced at Monty. "I'll deal with you in a moment, mage. Goodbye, Strong."

Monty formed a shield around me as Gault released another blue orb. This one was a blinding, blue-white ministar of death as it crashed into the shield and shredded it to nothing.

I cast the dawnward and saw Gault's orb slam into it and stop, before exploding with enough force to send me flying. I figured the only reason it didn't destroy me and my dawnward was because Monty's shield had slowed it down just enough to lose some power.

A second orb flanked Monty, moving faster than my eye could track, and buried itself in his ribs, shoving him to one side with a sick crunch as it broke bones.

Monty landed hard and coughed up blood as he got to his knees. He whispered something under his breath and formed golden symbols around me.

Gault's expression was one of outrage as he formed another blue orb of death. I crouched down and wrapped an arm around Peaches, putting my body in front of his.

"Simon!" Monty said, raising his voice, coughing up more blood in the process. "Your missile! Use it!"

"Are you insane? What is that going to do against him?"

"Do it! Now!" he yelled as he began to gesture. "Channel it through Ebonsoul!"

*"Ignis vitae!"* I yelled, directing all the energy within me through my blade and pointing it at Gault. If we were going to die, I was going to make the Keeper hurt while it happened.

A violet, gold, and black beam of energy seared through the air, crashing into Gault and launching him back into the rear of the Randy Rump with force. The look of shock on his face as he soared away was priceless, but we had no time to gloat.

The Darkanists had dropped their masks and were coming for us. Another explosion rocked the Rump as the area where Gault had landed grew bright with blue energy.

"Monty?" I said, pointing at the blue glow. "He's—"

"We're not staying," he said. "Hold on. This is going to be close."

Gault stood in the Rump, his body surrounded by blue orbs of destruction. His face looked calm but the madness was clear in his eyes.

"Shit, Monty," I said. "We need to go, now!"

"I can't leave a trail, or this will be pointless," Monty said. "A few seconds more."

Gault pointed in our direction and five orbs bore down on our position. I wrapped my arm around Peaches tighter and stared at Gault as death rushed at us.

"We don't have a few seconds."

"Yes...we do."

Monty formed a deep green circle around us and finished gesturing as the Randy Rump disappeared from sight. I swore I heard a scream of rage as we teleported away.

We reappeared on a barren plain in the middle of the night. Monty undid the circle with a slash, and it released a column of green energy into the starless sky.

"You did it," I said, turning to look at him. The blue lattice of energy was gone. "How did you do...Monty?"

"We...we made it," he rasped. "Found him."

His pale face was covered in sweat as he pointed ahead of us. He took a few steps and fell forward, unconscious.

In the distance, I saw a structure that resembled a small, stone cabin. There was no light inside and it looked about as deserted as the plain we stood in.

*Where is this place? Why did he bring us here?*

My hellhound rumbled at me, bringing me out of my thoughts.

"Monty," I said, crouching by his side as Peaches nudged me with his boulder of a head. "Help him, boy."

*<My saliva can heal him.>*

*<I know. Help him, boy. Hurry. Gault hit him with one of those deadly orbs.>*

Peaches sniffed the air and shook his head.

*<The bad energy is still inside the angry man.>*

*<We need to get it out. Can we get it out?>*

Peaches closed his eyes, focused, and took a deep breath. For a second, I thought he was going unleash one of his destructive barks, but he held the breath in and looked at me with glowing eyes. I had never seen him do that before, at least not like that.

*<Move back, bondmate.>*

*<Move back? Why do I need to...?>*

One moment my hellhound was standing next to a prone Monty; the next, he was standing over Monty and me. I looked up into my hellhound's enormous face and moved back.

He had gone XL and seemed to be larger than any of the

other times he had done it. My hellhound looked down at Monty, and I saw his eyes begin to glow brighter.

"What are you doing?" I called out. "I said help him, not blast him with your omega beams!"

<THE MAGE IS IN DIRE NEED OF ASSISTANCE. MY BALEFUL GLARE CAN NEGATE THE EFFECTS OF THE ORB HE WAS STRUCK WITH. PLEASE STEP BACK.>

I moved back and gave him plenty of room.

He looked down and focused his vision on Monty. Twin beams of red light cut into Monty's side with incredible precision. After a few seconds, a blue orb rose up into the air.

Peaches growled and the orb froze in place. The air around the orb shimmered with the power of his bark. My best guess was that he was holding the orb in place with the sound waves of his bark. With his baleful glare, he focused the two beams on the blue orb, blasting it to nothingness. He then refocused on Monty and looked at me.

<PLACE HIM ON HIS BACK, BONDMATE.>

I turned Monty over, trying to be gentle as possible as I moved him.

<EXPOSE THE WOUND.>

"Are you sure you know what you're doing?" I asked, concerned. "He still looks pretty bad."

Monty looked beyond bad. His face was still pale and covered in sweat. His chest rose and fell with each ragged breath, but it wasn't looking good. He actually looked worse.

<HE WILL GET WORSE IF I DON'T TEND TO HIS INJURY. PLEASE EXPOSE THE WOUND.>

I moved Monty's jacket and pulled up his shirt, exposing the wound where the orb had punched into his side. The area around the wound had turned an angry red with black lines of energy spider-webbing away from the entry site. They were slowly spreading up and around Monty's side.

"What is that?" I said, pointing at the lines. "The orb did that?"

<THE KEEPER ADDED AN ELEMENT OF POISON TO HIS ATTACK. WE MUST ACT WITH HASTE.>

Peaches stood over Monty and drooled on the wound. In seconds, the wound slowly sealed shut, but the black lines were still there. They had slowed down and then stopped. His entire side was covered with the black lines.

<I HAVE DONE ALL I CAN. YOU MUST DO THE REST.>

"I must *what*?" I asked, looking up at the massively ginormous head of my XL hellhound. "I'm not a healer. Do I look like a healer? How am I supposed to help him?"

<CALM DOWN.>

"Calm down?" I yelled. "Monty is dying and you expect me to do what? How am I going to stop whatever that is?" I pointed at black lines. "Those things are killing him."

<YOU SHARE BONDS WITH THE MAGE. THE BOND OF BROTHERHOOD, THE BOND OF POWER, THE BOND OF CREATION AND DEATH. THE ANSWER LIES IN YOUR BONDS.>

"I have no idea what you're talking about," I said, looking at the unconscious Monty. "The bond of brotherhood I understand—what bond of power and creation?"

<YOU SHARE A STORMBLOOD AND YOU SHARE THE FIRST ELDER RUNE. YOU MUST USE THESE BONDS TO SAVE HIM. IF YOU FAIL, HE WILL DIE. I HAVE ONLY SLOWED THE PROCESS. YOU MUST STOP AND REVERSE IT.>

"How am I supposed to do that?" I asked, frustrated and confused. "Where the hell are we? There's nothing here to help. We're in the middle of nowhere."

<EVERYTHING YOU NEED IS WITHIN. USE WHAT YOU POSSESS.>

"Don't you get all cryptic on me now," I said. "The last thing I need right now are riddles. Use what I possess?"

<YES. YOU HAVE THE MEANS TO HEAL THE MAGE.>

"I have the means?" I asked, wracking my brain. "I can't cast a stormblood on my own. I'm not a mage, I can't help him. He's going to die."

<ONLY IF YOU DO NOTHING. USE YOUR WEAPON. HURRY.>

"Use my weapon?" I asked. "What good is Grim Whisper going to do?"

He stared at me and chuffed, shaking his head.

<YOUR BLADE, BONDMATE. USE YOUR BLADE.>

I focused and formed Ebonsoul.

It gleamed with an inner light as the runes along its length fluctuated from violet to red to gold, and then darkened to black, only to start the rotation over again.

I stood there focused on my blade and let my senses expand. We stood in a plane of nothingness. As far as I could sense, it was just Monty, Peaches, and me.

<YOU KNOW THE WORDS. LET THEM COME.>

"I'm glad someone knows the words, because I certainly don't," I said. "How am I supposed to know the words?"

<STOP TALKING AND LISTEN.>

Great—now I was getting attitude from my super-smart hellhound.

I knelt down next to Monty, and held Ebonsoul close to the wound. I didn't know what I expected. Stabbing him with my blade would only make things worse. I didn't need to siphon energy from him; I needed to heal him somehow. The frustration and fear made me want to scream.

I knew I had to do something, anything.

I closed my eyes, took a deep breath and grounded myself, letting my senses expand again. I connected to everything around me, searching and feeling for the bonds. I felt the overly large presence of my hellhound, the fading energy signature of Monty and the energy pulsing through my body, through the blade I held in my hand.

There, deep inside Ebonsoul—the words I needed were there.

"*Sana animam*," the words escaped my lips in a whisper at first. "*Sana animam!*"

I felt the tug of energy from my body rush down my arm and into Ebonsoul. It formed a violet-and-gold beam, which flowed outward and gently covered Monty in a cloud of energy. I looked down at the wound and saw the black lines of death slowly disappear from Monty's side.

"I did it," I managed as a weight of exhaustion came over me. "What...what did I do?"

After a few seconds, I saw the same black lines appear on my hand. They started creeping up my arm and a bracing cold enveloped my body. I was about to warn my hellhound to get away when the world turned sideways and went dark.

# FOURTEEN

"What happened?" I managed as I opened my eyes in a dimly lit room. "Where are we? What happened?"

"You saved my life," Monty said, looking down at his shredded shirt. "My shirt, not so much. Nevertheless, thank you."

"Sorry about the shirt," I said and made to sit up. The room tilted to one side and convinced me it was a bad idea. I put my head down again and waited for the room to settle down. "Whoa, I'm just going to lay down here for a few months if you don't mind."

Monty extended a hand and helped me up before offering me a cup of golden liquid. I sniffed the liquid and realized it had a distinct, non-coffee smell.

"*This* is not javambrosia," I said, scrunching my nose at the cup. "What is it?"

"It's not coffee, but it *will* restore you," he said, pushing the cup in my hand toward me. "Drink it slowly, drink it all, and let it work."

I took a sip from the cup, and the golden liquid warmed

me immediately as it went down. It had a strong taste of honey and lemon tea.

"What is this?" I said suspiciously. "Are you trying to make me drink tea?"

"I wouldn't dare. It's a healing elixir I learned from Quan," he said. "From what I could tell, you somehow managed to neutralize the poison in my system, while sharing some of your life force. How did you do this?"

I extended my hand and saw that the black lines were gone.

"I don't know," I said. "Stress? You were dying, and my hellhound told me I could save you with Ebonsoul. I figured if it was poison, it could do something after what Orethe did to it. I'm glad it worked."

"Whatever that orb was, it was one of the deadliest casts I have experienced," Monty said. "The poison was incredibly debilitating and fast-acting. If you hadn't acted as quickly as you had, we wouldn't be having this conversation."

"That poison was nasty," I said, looking down at my hands. "It was in me. Right before I passed out, I saw it in my hands."

"It's what caused you to lose consciousness," he said. "The poison overwhelmed your body's defenses. Whatever necrotic properties Ebonsoul now possesses seem to have passed to your curse. You should be dead, but somehow your curse prevented your demise, and your blade effectively neutralized the poison in my body."

"It wasn't just me," I said, taking another sip of the elixir. "It was Ebonsoul and Peaches." I motioned to him with my cup. "He lasered the orb out of you and then slobbered you with his saliva."

Peaches' ears perked up at the mention of his name. He was back to regular size and rumbled as I looked at him. I rubbed his head as he chuffed at me. Monty glanced down at my hellhound and nodded.

"You have my gratitude, Mighty One," he said and formed a large sausage, which he offered to my hellhound. The sausage disappeared from sight an instant later. "Thank you."

*<Tell the angry man I would be more thankful if he made me another sausage.>*

*<Absolutely not. Eat your meat and be happy.>*

"He says thank you," I said, raising the cup of healing, honey tea to my lips.

I finished the rest of the elixir and examined the interior of the cabin.

It was much larger on the inside; I saw a fully equipped kitchen to my left with an adjoining hallway which led to more rooms it seemed.

I currently sat on a small, sturdy futon in the large living room, which was amply furnished with several chairs, a small table, and a fireplace. Violet flame was currently keeping the space warm, but not overheating it.

Every wall in this room was covered with bookcases. I glanced at the books and gave up trying to read the titles. Most were written in a language I had no hope of understanding; I knew they were runes of some kind, but none that I had ever seen before.

"We can't beat him," I said, keeping my voice low. "He barely broke a sweat and nearly killed us. If you hadn't ported us out of there when you did—"

"I know," Monty said. "My uncle warned us, but I thought he was being dramatic. This was one of the few times he was actually underselling the situation. Gault is too strong for us."

"How do we stop him?" I asked. "Is this the moment where we call in the big guns?"

"There are no big guns to call," Monty said, taking the cup from me. "We have to deal with this."

"What are you talking about?" I asked, confused. "We can start with Dex and the Morrigan, follow that up with LD, TK, and the rest of the Ten. Hell, we can even send out a call to Hades and the Midnight Echelon. What do you mean there are no big guns? I just named more than fifteen, if we can assemble all of the Ten. I mean, I would be okay with just LD and TK, but if we can get all of them..."

He waited for me to finish and shook his head.

"You don't understand," he said. "It's not that I don't want to. Every cell in my body is telling me to employ assistance for this—we are grossly outmatched—but we can't. We *can't* call them for this."

"You're right, I don't understand," I said. "Explain it to me, and use small, non-magical words."

"The only reason we're still alive is because of the First Elder Rune," he said. "Despite being immensely powerful, no one you named—with the exception of my uncle, the Morrigan, and Hades—would stand a chance against Gault."

"The Ten?"

"Not even the Ten," he said. "I think my uncle was trying to convey this to me, but I didn't understand at the time. It's not that he doesn't want to help, it's that he can't."

I shook my head in disbelief.

"But...they are powerful," I said. "They can fight him. You saw what he did to us. We can't face him alone. We can't face him at all. Are you saying they aren't strong enough to take on the Keeper?"

"No," Monty said, "they have the power, but we have the rune. It gives us a distinct advantage and a certain level of protection. His first attack should have seriously injured us. It sent me through a glass facade, yet I emerged unscathed."

"I thought you shielded yourself."

"There was no time to shield myself," he explained. "No, that was a defensive property of the First Elder Rune."

"But we can't face Gault," I said. "Did you see how he manhandled us? We can't stop that."

"And yet you must," a voice said from the other side of the room. "To directly involve those you named would doom most of them to a painful death."

"You?" I said, looking at the man sitting across the room. "What are *you* doing here?"

"I could ask you the same thing."

I turned to Monty.

"You found him? How?"

"The First Elder Rune," Monty said, turning to face the man. "I had been working on a solution to locating him for some time, before I realized I held the answer all along."

"I didn't anticipate you would be able to use the rune to locate me," the man said. "You shouldn't have been able to find me—but you are after all, your uncle's nephew. I underestimated your ability, but I can't say I'm surprised."

It was Evergreen.

He was wearing a loose-fitting, rust-colored linen shirt and dark slacks. He still had a beard, which was more salt than pepper relative to when I saw him last.

"How are you still alive?" I asked. "Lotus told us—"

"You spoke to the Lotus?" Evergreen asked. "Is she still alive?"

"She sort of asked the same thing about you."

"Yes, she is still alive," Monty said. "I have placed her in an interstice. Gault won't find her there, at least for some time."

"That must have infuriated Gault," Evergreen said with a small laugh. "I'm sure he didn't take that well."

"He tried to kill us and nearly succeeded," I said. "I'd say he's pretty pissed off, yes."

"You're blocking him somehow, aren't you?" Monty asked. "How?"

"I may have shared the First Elder Rune with you, but I still retain limited access to the other runes," he said. "As you can see, I'm not quite dead, just diminished."

"Are you dying?" I asked, concerned. "I don't mean in the distant future, centuries from now. I mean in the near, next few hours kind of immediate future."

"Simon..." Monty chastised me. "He's still the Arch Keeper. He deserves a modicum of respect."

"There has been no insult," Evergreen said, raising a hand. "No, I'm not dying, at least as far as I can tell. Why do you ask?"

"Lotus thought that sharing the First Elder Rune meant you should be dead or dying," I replied. "But your access to the other runes is keeping you alive? Is that it?"

"Something like that," he said. "It's why I removed myself from your plane. My presence there without my rune would disrupt—"

"The balance," Monty said. "Has it been—?"

"The balance remains," Evergreen said, looking past us and off into the distance. "Even now with Gault trying his best to tip the scales in his favor, the balance remains. He never did understand how everything is interconnected."

"Good, then we can give you your rune back now."

"Can you?" Evergreen asked, sounding mildly amused. "If so, I'm ready to receive it from you."

"And I'm ready to give it back," I said, glancing at Monty. "Make with the finger-wiggles, and give the Keeper his rune back."

Monty stared at me and shook his head.

"I wouldn't even know where to begin," he said. "We can't give it back yet."

"What are you talking about? Just do the reverse of whatever it was he did to give it to us. That should do it. Right?"

"You are certainly becoming strong enough," Evergreen

said, looking at us. "But you're not quite there...yet. Aside from that, you still haven't reconciled your beliefs."

"I'm reconciled."

"Are you, really?"

"I think we both agree and believe that this rune is better with you," I said, glancing at Monty. "There, reconciled. Take back your rune."

"It's not quite that easy," Evergreen said with a small smile. "I understand your reluctance to carry this burden, I truly do, but I want you to think about this situation objectively. Why do you still have the rune?"

"Because *you* gave it to us?" I answered, getting upset. "What kind of question is that?"

Evergreen remained smiling, but didn't answer.

"Wait," Monty said. "Why didn't Gault remove the rune when he had us in front of him?"

"Because he was focused on pounding us to death in that moment?"

"No, he should have been able to eliminate us with ease," Monty said. "Why didn't he? How protected are we?"

"*That* is the right question," Evergreen said, then turned to me. "I have another for you: are you a dark immortal?"

"No! It hasn't happened and it's not going to happen," I said with an audible sigh of frustration. "I wish people would drop it already with the darkness. If I'm a dark immortal, then Monty is the darkest of all mages, and I know for a fact he isn't."

Evergreen glanced at Monty and nodded.

"He is *not* the darkest of all mages, though there is some darkness in all of us, wouldn't you admit?"

"I would," I said. "We all have *some* darkness. That doesn't mean I'm becoming a dark immortal."

"Tristan," Evergreen said, "do you have the answer to your earlier question?"

"Because he couldn't take it," Monty said. "He doesn't have the First Elder Rune because he couldn't take it from us."

Evergreen nodded.

"What is the role of the Lotus?" Evergreen asked. "Why is she important?"

"She is a vessel?"

Evergreen nodded again.

"Continue. Why does he need her?" Evergreen asked. "Why is she important to him?"

"He can't take the rune from us by force, but if he ends us, she can hold it for him, and then he can take it from her?"

"Close," Evergreen said. "In order to get the rune from you two, he will need to form a conduit between himself and the First Elder Rune. How will he do that?"

"He needs to kill us?"

"No," Evergreen said. "You must be alive to transfer the rune, at least initially. Think—what has he told you about the Lotus? What is her purpose?"

"To die for him," I said. "He said he created her, and her purpose was to die for him."

"The First Elder Rune must have a host," Evergreen said. "If he had killed you, it would have been lost to him without a conduit present to hold it."

"Wait... He can't take it from us, but he can release it from us?"

"Death has a way of making us release the things we hold on to," Evergreen answered. "The First Elder Rune will not inhabit a lifeless body."

"If he kills us, where would it go?" I asked, really not enjoying this whole subject. "Wouldn't it just go back to you?"

"No," Evergreen said. "Where would it go, Tristan?"

"The next Keeper in rotation," Monty said, "unless it

could be intercepted. Gault knows how to intercept the transfer, doesn't he?"

"The Lotus," Evergreen said. "She is more than a vessel. She is a conduit."

"Are you saying she can hold the First Elder Rune?"

"For a brief moment, yes," Evergreen admitted. "If she has the rune, and Gault siphons her life force—"

"He gets the rune?"

"And access to all five," Evergreen said. "He will then usher in his age of entropy."

"About that," I said. "How long have you known that he was batshit insane? He wants to undo everything just to remake it again in a way that he thinks is best. He wants to create a magical paradise where everyone is a mage?"

"He is wrong," Monty said. "His vision is warped and twisted."

"I thought you would be amenable to his vision, Tristan," Evergreen said. "Didn't you say that the magical knowledge regarding the runes should be disseminated freely?"

"Not at the expense of the lives of everyone on the plane," Monty said. "That cost is too high. Even if it's one life, the cost is too high."

"Do you agree with this, Simon?"

"I like the idea of making it an even playing field," I said. "When everyone is powerful, then no one is. The problem is that it's never evenly spread out. Gault said it himself. He would have to *instruct and guide*. I'm pretty sure that if anyone stood against him, that would quickly become *crush and kill*."

"Then what is the greater good?" Evergreen said. "How do you resolve this situation?"

"You said we have to get stronger to give you the rune back," I said. "So we can't give it back to you. At least not yet."

"True," Evergreen answered. "Is there another outcome, then?"

"Giving Gault the rune is out of the question," Monty said. "The only other solution is to keep the rune."

"You want us to keep the rune that is going to get us killed, and if not killed, hunted by everyone?"

"Not everyone," Monty said. "There are some who would stand with us."

"Whom we would get killed, according to you," I said. "The solution is to get stronger and give it back, after we stop Gault from trying to break everything."

"How do you propose we do that?" Monty asked. "I'm open to suggestions. I'd prefer to give the rune back before we suffer any negative side effects."

"How do we get stronger?" I asked, looking at Evergreen. "I know you know."

"I do and so do you," he said. "I've just given you the answer."

"You what?" I said, thinking back to his words and coming up with nothing. "When?"

"When I explained how Gault would transfer the rune," he said. "The solution you need is there. Right now, you are the catalyst, and Tristan is the rune-bearer. It's one rune, split in two. You need to—"

"Establish the balance," Monty finished. "We need to make the rune whole. I thought only a Keeper could hold an intact Elder Rune."

"There have been exceptions...depending on the method used."

"What are you saying?" I asked. "You think Monty can hold the entire Elder Rune on his own?"

"He has most of it now," Evergreen said. "You possess the catalyst, but he holds the bulk of the rune. I'd say he's managed to do so without any ill effects, wouldn't you?"

"This is why you split it," Monty said, staring at Evergreen. "You anticipated this."

"I've lived a long time," Evergreen answered with a short nod. "I learned to see a few steps ahead."

"It's too much power. It will burn right through me," Monty said. "I have no way to wield that much power without tearing myself apart."

"True," Evergreen said, "unless you contain the power, that is."

"I don't know how to do that," Monty said. "Even if I could somehow rejoin the rune, I wouldn't know how to contain it inside of me."

"No one said it needed to be rejoined right this moment," Evergreen said. "But you *can* contain it."

"It would require knowledge I don't currently possess," Monty replied. "A containment cast of that caliber is beyond me."

"Think, Tristan. Instead of focusing on what you don't have or know, focus on what you do," Evergreen said. "How can you make it whole? You two were not chosen for this by accident."

Monty grew pensive, then shook his head as he stared at Evergreen.

"No," Monty said, "that can't be it."

"What can't be it?" I asked, concerned at the tone of his voice. "What is it?"

"There is one way to make the rune whole," Monty said. "The First Elder Rune won't inhabit a lifeless body."

"I got that part. That's what he said," I answered. "How is that a problem?"

Then the realization hit me.

"It's the only way," Evergreen said. "Unless you can think of another?"

"That's why you chose us," I said. "How long have you been planning this?"

"Not as long as you would think," Evergreen said, looking away. "Certain situations had to be nudged into place. There were a few moments that relied on your free will as well."

"My free will? Really?" I snapped. "Because I've been feeling like a piece on a board ever since I stepped into this world of magic and gods."

"I can assure you, no undue influence was used on your choices," Evergreen assured me. "You have presented a confluence of opportunities ever since Kali cursed you alive."

"Since Kali cursed me?"

"Yes," he said. "A cursed immortal is not a normal occurrence. The fatality rate is quite high for human-to-immortal transformations. Frankly, I fully expected you to die within minutes of your curse. It usually proves too powerful and disassembles the human in question."

"Are you saying Kali was trying to kill me?"

"No," he said, shaking his head. "Out of everyone, I think Kali knew you would survive. It's why she marked you, why she watches you so closely. You have slowly become her favored one."

"She has a funny way of showing my favored status," I said. "How does that make us the choice for what's going on?"

"Tristan is on the verge of ascending to Archmage in a few shifts," Evergreen said, glancing at Monty. "He already holds elder runes. This has just accelerated the process. And, well, you..."

"Have a hard time staying dead."

"I was going to say, again, that you have been cursed alive," Evergreen clarified. "You can facilitate the catalyst rejoining the First Elder Rune."

"You said it would kill him," I said, looking at an angry Monty. "He's not strong enough."

"As I said, there have been exceptions," Evergreen answered. "If he can contain it, harness the power, then he can survive. If not, he will die."

"This solution truly sucks."

"I didn't choose this situation because it was elegant," Evergreen said with an edge. "I chose it because it was implausible and difficult to understand. Finding an accomplished mage with the required potential who is also bonded to a cursed immortal wasn't exactly easy or common."

"What was plan B?" I asked, still not convinced this was the only way to go. "What if you didn't have us?"

"War," Evergreen said. "A war between Keepers that would devastate and destroy several planes, including yours. The loss of life would be staggering. Some of the planes would be uninhabitable after the protracted conflict."

"How could you know?" I asked. "Have the Keepers gone to war before?"

"Yes," Evergreen said, his voice somber. "An act I don't intend on repeating. If it means I must risk my life along with yours to save the trillions that would be lost in a War of Keepers, then I will—as many times as necessary."

"What do we need to do?" Monty said, his voice determined. "Show me what I need to do to contain the First Elder Rune."

"I can show you what you must do, but the risk is great," Evergreen said. "There are no guarantees here. We are entering uncharted territory. You're not even an Archmage. The containment cast alone could undo you."

"I only run the risk of death if we are successful," Monty said, and then turned to me. "Simon has to die in order for us to even have a chance to be successful. It's his choice first."

I stared hard at Evergreen.

"Can you really show him how to contain the rune?" I

asked. "Not the theory, the actual cast. I'm not going to die just so you can kill Monty in this insane plan."

"On my word as a Keeper and a mage, I will bring all of my remaining ability to bear in assisting Tristan's containment of the First Elder Rune," Evergreen said, seriously, "even if it means I must sacrifice my own life in the process."

A wave of power flowed through the cabin at his words, reinforcing the oath Evergreen had just made. He looked at me and nodded. I returned the nod, absolutely sure that he would do whatever it took to guarantee we had a chance at stopping Gault and his twisted plan.

"I believe you," I said with a nod of my own. "What about my bond with my hellhound? If I'm gone, won't he become unstoppable and attack you?"

"I will forestall the effects of the temporary severing of your bond," Evergreen said. "Your curse should return you to us before my hold on your bond is broken."

"And if it doesn't?"

"You will be dead, as in a final death," he said, glancing at Monty. "Mage Montague will join you shortly after, obliterated by the power of the rune, and I don't suppose I would last much longer than he against an unbound hellhound at my current state of power."

"Don't try to boost my morale all at once now," I said. "What is it with you mages and your anti-morale pep talks?"

"There is one silver lining," Evergreen said. "It's not the best of outcomes if we fail in containment, but the First Elder Rune would be trapped here, in this place, with what remains of us until the next rotation of the Arch Keeper. Gault would be stopped."

"Not destroyed?"

"No. We would be denying him access to the key to his plan, but he would still exist."

"And we would all be dead. Even my hellhound?"

"Yes, he would be trapped here." he answered, after a brief pause. "I don't know how long a hellhound can survive without food, especially a puppy like yours. But eventually, even your hellhound would lose his life, too. As I said, not the best of outcomes."

"But Gault wouldn't get the rune," I said. "We would stop him and his genocidal psychoplan."

Evergreen nodded.

"Fine. What's a little death when everything I know is at risk?" I said with a crooked grin. "I swear I'll come back and kill you if I end up permanently dead."

"Of course," Evergreen said, matching my grin before looking at Monty. "Tristan, are you ready?"

"Not in the slightest," he said. "Not that it matters one bit. Show me what I need to do."

"Watch me," Evergreen said, making his way to stand in the middle of the floor. "Do exactly as I do. This cast will demand all of your focus and concentration."

Evergreen began to gesture and form a circle.

# FIFTEEN

Peaches and I moved away from the center of the floor as Evergreen created a large, pulsing white circle of power. Together with Monty he stepped into it as they began casting symbols into the air around them.

Evergreen would trace a series of symbols, and Monty would repeat them. Each time, Evergreen would correct some detail of the symbol that Monty traced, and then repeat the process.

It took several tries before Monty started getting the hang of the complicated symbols the Keeper was tracing in the air between them, and once he did, they would move on to a more complicated one. Each symbol looked harder than the previous one. They kept at this until the symbols were looking like intersecting lines of energy I couldn't understand.

I glanced down at my hellhound, took a deep breath, and let it out slow.

I figured I should prepare him for what was coming. If he saw me get dusted, there was a good chance that his next thought would be to tear, blast, and bark through whoever did the dusting.

That would be a bad situation.

I had no idea what would happen if our bond was completely broken, since it required death to sever the bond between us now. I could only imagine it would be the worst of all worlds.

My hellhound was nearly indestructible as he was now. If he transformed into a rampaging hellhound beast, or worse, a rampaging XL hellhound beast, I doubted Evergreen and Monty combined could so much as slow him down before he tore them apart and ended them.

It was the first time I realized how much of a threat a hellhound could be. Part of me now understood why people and the beings we encountered defaulted to fear when they saw him.

The other part of me still saw him as my hellhound puppy who was eternally starving. A hellhound had the potential to be a devastating force of death—if he wasn't busy chomping down on a massive sausage, that is.

I crouched down and rubbed his ginormous head. He chuffed in response and nudged my hand back to his ears.

*<Hey, boy. We need to talk.>*

How do you tell your bondmate you need to die?

*<Is the angry man going to make me more meat? My saliva saved him.>*

*<It did.>*

*<It's not easy being this mighty. I need energy. I'm starving.>*

I smiled and suddenly realized just how hard this was going to be.

*<I have to tell you something. Can we focus on something else besides your stomach and meat for a few minutes?>*

*<Something else besides meat? Why? Meat is life.>*

There was no easy way to say this, so I opted for trying the ripping-off-the-bandaid method, failing horribly to find the words.

*\<I have to go away for a little while.\>*

He stared up into my eyes. For a brief moment, I thought I saw confusion. Then he shook his head and nudged my hand again.

*\<Wherever you go, I go. You are my bondmate.\>*

*\<You can't go where I'm going.\>*

*\<Why not? You are my bondmate. I go where you go.\>*

*\<Not this time. This time I have to go far away, where you can't go.\>*

*\<There is no place you can go that I can't go.\>*

I closed my eyes and placed my forehead against his head. This was too hard to explain. It was too hard...period. If things went wrong, this would be the last time I saw my hellhound. How could I tell him that?

*\<You are sad. Why are you sad? Do you need meat? You can ask the angry man to make you meat. If you ate some meat, it would make you happy.\>*

A small laugh erupted from my chest at his suggestion of my needing more meat. I took another deep breath, looked away, and wiped my eyes as I let it out. I felt a hand on my shoulder and Evergreen looked down at me.

I saw Monty still in the circle, working on his containment cast.

"Let me help," Evergreen said, placing a hand on Peaches' head and my shoulder. A few moments later, his hands gave off a golden glow, and I felt a shudder of energy go through my body. "That should make it easier. Tell him the truth."

"What did you do?"

"I merely made it easier for him to communicate, and for you to understand," he said, heading back to Monty. "He is your bondmate, but you are still too young to communicate on his level. This will make it easier, without necessitating an increase in his size. Don't delay; the cast won't last long, and our time here grows short."

He walked back to the circle and began speaking to Monty again. I turned to Peaches and let out another breath.

<Hey, boy. I have something to tell you.>

<You need to go somewhere where I cannot follow. From your expression and the inflection of your words, and since there is no place on this or any plane where I cannot follow you, I can only surmise you mean you must travel somewhere that can only be reached by your death.>

<Yes? How are you doing this? You're speaking like you're XL, but you're normal sized.>

<It would appear that the cast executed by the Keeper is facilitating our communication. Do you really have to die?>

<Yes. I have a part of the First Elder Rune, and we're going to try and make the entire rune whole. That means I need to give my part to Monty.>

<Why does this require your death? Isn't the Keeper strong enough to transfer the part you have?>

<Not the way he is now. He's not strong enough.>

<He should eat more meat. Protein is essential to power.>

<I'll make sure to let him know. We're kind of forcing this situation; it is dangerous, and I don't know if I'm coming back. This could be the last time we see each other.>

<I am saddened by this news. You are my bondmate, and I anticipated spending all my days by your side. This also means that my life, too, will be coming to an end. It is only fitting, since our bond will be broken. I will revert to a mindless creature of destruction, worthy of death.>

<No. Evergreen will keep our bond intact for as long as possible.>

<Why? He would only be prolonging the inevitable. To keep my bond intact without my bondmate is pointless. I will not and cannot form another bond with someone else.>

<You do realize Kali cursed me, right?>

<I am aware the blue goddess doesn't like you very much. What does she have to do with this?>

<She cursed me alive. Which means—at least in theory—that if I die, I will come back.>

<Has this theory been tested?>

<Well, Dahvina killed me once, but that was under controlled circumstances. I was dead for three hours.>

<You did not remain dead.>

<Kali's curse prevents me from dying permanently. I can die, I just don't stay that way. It's not fun, which is why I try to avoid it as much as possible.>

<You can't avoid it now, though.>

I looked over to where Evergreen and Monty stood, focused on the symbols in front of them. Evergreen nodded as Monty kept creating the same symbol. A few times Evergreen would whisper something or point, and Monty would adjust the symbol.

I shook my head slowly.

<I can't. Not this time.>

<But you will come back?>

<I don't know, but I really hope so. Kali is kind of a big deal in the power department, being a goddess. I'm figuring her curse will bring me back.>

<And if it doesn't?>

<Then I wanted to say goodbye. You were the best hellhound I could ever know.>

<You only know two, and my sire doesn't count. I am the best hellhound you know because I am the only hellhound you know.>

<True, and your sire has not been called mighty like you. Thank you for being my amazing bondmate and saving me as many times as you have.>

<I am your bondmate. No thanks are needed. How will you die?
>

<I'm pretty sure Evergreen has it figured out. Come on—it looks like Monty has the containment cast down.>

I walked over to where Monty and Evergreen stood with

Peaches by my side. Monty recreated the cast several more times before Evergreen nodded in satisfaction.

"You have the containment cast," Evergreen said. "Once the catalyst rejoins the main rune, you must contain the First Elder Rune immediately. You will have seconds at most."

"And Simon?" Monty asked. "What will happen to him?"

"Simon will hopefully be working his way back to the realm of the living while you are containing the rune," Evergreen said, glancing at me. "Kali does not work in half measures. If she has cursed you alive, this should work."

"But you're not sure?" I asked.

Evergreen turned to me and shook his head.

"I possess many milennia of knowledge," he said. "This is uncharted territory even for me. Kali's marked are not usually immortal, which is why you are an anomaly. I truly do not know what will happen after your demise."

"That makes two of us," I said. "The last time I was killed, it was only for a short time—three hours. I haven't been eager to revisit death since then."

"Do you recall anything that could be helpful from that incident?"

"Not really. It was painful, but that was probably because Dahvina needed to do some untangling with my bonds," I said. "Other than that, it's mostly a blank."

He examined me and nodded.

"It would seem we will all be learning something new today," Evergreen said, gesturing and forming another circle, this one a deep violet. "Tristan, please remain in your circle and prepare. I will assist Simon in his death."

"Well, when you put it that way, it almost sounds gentle."

"I can assure you, it will not be," Evergreen warned. "I have the general concept, but it will tax me beyond my current capabilities. I will have to interrupt Kali's curse and stop your bodily functions long enough for you to die."

"Sounds simple enough," I said. "Interrupt the curse and take me out. How hard can that be?"

"If I could stop time, it would be child's play," he replied. "Since I do not possess that ability, it will be a monumentally difficult task, even for me. Kali's curse will fight me every step of the way. In addition to preventing it from taking effect and bringing you back immediately, I will need to maintain the bond you have with your hellhound intact to prevent his transformation."

"Can you pull this off?" I asked, looking at the violet circle. "I mean, can you *really* pull this off?"

"Does it matter?" he said with a small smile. "We aren't exactly tripping over options here. I will do everything I can to make sure you have every opportunity to return. Most of this rests with Kali and her curse. If I were you, I'd be asking for her favor right about now."

"We're not friendly like that," I said. "She kind of hates me."

"Pity," he said, shaking out his hands. "We'll do what we can with what we have, then. Ready?"

"Am I ready for you to end my life?"

"At least—and hopefully—temporarily, yes."

A strange calm came over me. There had been plenty of times Monty and I faced death, or some creature or being promising us death. This time, though, it wasn't coming from someone trying to kill me because I was standing in their way.

This time it was to save everything.

I nodded.

"As ready as I will ever be."

He motioned for me to enter the violet circle. I looked over to where Monty stood. He gave me a short nod which I returned.

"Don't think this means you can lounge in your death,"

Monty said, staring at me intently. "Make sure you get back as soon as possible."

"Will do," I said, rubbing my hellhound's oversized head one last time before stepping into the violet circle. I stared at Evergreen. "Make sure nothing happens to either of them. This is my family."

Evergreen nodded and began gesturing.

# SIXTEEN

White and gold symbols flowed from Evergreen's fingers.

I heard Peaches whine as the symbols entered the violet circle I stood in, and I saw Monty begin to gesture as his white circle increased in intensity. After a few seconds, the violet energy around me did the same, growing too bright for me to see clearly out of the circle.

More golden-white symbols flowed into the circle and surrounded my body. They hovered around me for several seconds before descending on me. I suddenly felt heavy, and my chest became tight. Pain bloomed in my shoulder and raced down my arm.

A cold sweat covered my brow, and I could briefly see Evergreen, both arms outstretched, exerting himself as the runes kept flowing out of his fingers. His face was covered in sweat as he whispered words under his breath.

I saw Peaches sitting on his haunches next to Evergreen. The runes on his flanks beginning to become brighter as he kept his gaze focused on me.

A sudden overwhelming fatigue descended on me, and all I wanted was to lay down and take a nap. I tried to take a deep breath and found that the most I could manage was a shallow half-breath. The floor see-sawed, and I fell to one knee, trying to hold onto my balance. Whatever was still in my stomach threatened to exit my body forcibly as a powerful wave of nausea gripped me.

I fell forward and came to the realization that I was having a heart attack. The cool floor of the cabin caressed my cheek as I understood that I was dying. I took one last look at Monty, Peaches, and Evergreen before closing my eyes, leaving them and the cabin behind.

I opened my eyes and gazed upon a black, marble floor. It was polished to a high sheen and reflected the ceiling. I lay still for a few minutes, taking everything in.

That's when the pain arrived.

*How can I be feeling pain if I'm dead?*

The logical answer was that Kali was a sadistic, evil goddess that delighted in my moments of pain. Agony has a way of clouding your thinking. Rational thought flies right out the window when searing pain has you in its grip.

*Get over yourself. You may be her Marked One, but she barely notices your existence.*

More pain squeezed my head, giving me the migraine from hell, as a vise grip of agony compressed my temples. My vision tunneled in as everything around me became hidden in a gray fog.

My muscles felt like they were being peeled back with ample applications of hydrochloric acid poured over them to heighten the torture. I tried screaming, but no sound escaped my lips.

An immense pressure followed the acid bath, crushing me; it felt as if someone had dropped an elephant on my back. The pressure continued until I felt it would crush me to nothingness, leaving only a pile of dust where I was lying.

The pressure subsided and I was able to breathe again for

a moment, right before my lungs inhaled napalm. Everything inside me burned. I looked down at myself and realized I wasn't melting, even though it felt that way. I curled into the fetal position as tears streamed down my face and the indescribable torture wracked my body.

"Just kill me already," I rasped. "Stop this, please."

"Why would I repeat what you have already done?" a familiar voice said. "I cannot kill that which is already dead."

Kali.

"This...this wasn't me," I said, my voice hoarse. "I didn't do this."

"Are you saying the Keeper killed you against your will?"

"No... This was the only way...I mean, I had to..."

The pain snatched my thoughts away.

"Focus," she said, her voice hard. "It is only pain. You should be intimately familiar with it, the way a lover knows all of the contours of his beloved's body."

"I don't think....I don't think I ever want to get *that* familiar with pain."

"Which is why you keep experiencing it this way," she said. "Let go. Stop resisting it. What's the worst it can do? Kill you? You've crossed that threshold, haven't you?"

I heard the smile in her voice.

Lifting my head felt impossible at the moment. The smooth floor was cool against my skin as I took several deep breaths and surrendered to the immense pain in my body.

I sensed her energy signature all around me, and then felt it compress itself to one point not too far away from where I lay.

I managed to catch a glimpse of her feet from my prone position as she crossed the marble floor. The space around her warped and shifted as she approached my location. Everything seemed to settle once she stopped walking and crouched down to look me in the face.

I looked up into her face, and even the small act of moving my eyes to gaze at her face drove hot nails of agony into my brain.

She smiled and shook her head.

"Why are you holding onto this pain?" she asked, still gazing down at me. "Let it go. Not everything needs to be suffering, you know. Joy, pleasure, and happiness are excellent alternatives to suffering."

"You want...you want me to find joy in my pain?"

"Pain, like cold and heat, are merely sensory inputs," she said. "Suffering and feelings of agony require a shift in response. They are reactions to the inputs, just like joy and happiness. It is all relative."

"I can't find joy in this."

"But you can—and must," she said. "The blind man would revel in the blazing light of the midday sun that is cursed by the sighted man. The light is the same; only the response differs. It is the same with pain."

I remained silent, took a few deep breaths, and glanced down at the floor. It took me a few seconds to get my bearings through the pain. I realized from the reflection on the floor that I was lying in the center of an immense temple. All of the walls were decorated with ornate and intricate stone carvings of Kali in various poses of battle or dance.

The ceiling itself was a staggering work of sculpted art, detailed with scenes of worship and dancing. If I focused on any one section, it would begin to move slowly, demonstrating complicated dances as I watched in awe.

Even through the haze of the pain, I understood that this place was special—and it slowly dawned on me that no human hands had made it.

"Where...where am I?" I asked, my voice hoarse. "What is this place?"

"Rise," she said, and I felt the pain diminish. "Sit."

"What did you do?" I asked as the pain slowly left me. "How did you do that?"

"I did nothing," she answered. "The moment you were able to focus on something other than your pain, it diminished and lost its hold over you."

She was right. As soon as I had noticed the stonework, the pain had fallen to the background of my mind. Even now, it was becoming a distant memory.

Unsteadily, I got to my knees and noticed the large cushion next to me. She walked over to sit across from me on a cushion similar to mine, except where mine was an explosion of different colors, her cushion was black and edged with gold and red elements.

I managed to sink into my cushion, losing what little dignity I had left as I tumbled into its center. After some contortions, I found my balance and sat properly, crossing my legs and keeping my back straight. I faced her as she descended effortlessly into hers.

I took a moment to look around.

This place was similar to the mandir I had visited in New Jersey, on a scale that boggled my imagination. I immediately knew this was no temple sitting in New Jersey somewhere. The carvings in the walls still moved eerily when I focused on them, and became still when I didn't. The stonework of the temple was a mixture of deep violets, bright reds, vibrant greens, brilliant blues, and amazing yellows.

It was unlike any place I had ever seen. The temple itself felt alive. I half expected the lifelike figures from the walls to peel off their pedestals and dance their way to me. Every time I moved my head, the black marble floor glistened with silver afterimages out of the corner of my eyes.

The entire space pulsed with a hidden power which thrummed through me. My body felt as if I sat on an enormous tuning fork that had just been hit. The low vibration around me was impossible to ignore as it wrapped itself around me with a low hum.

For a few more moments, I sat in complete silence, marveling at the wonder of this place.

"What is this place?" I asked, my voice hushed—whether out of fear or awe, I had no way of telling. I figured it was a bit of both. "It's amazing."

"You seem to have matured somewhat, my Cursed."

"Dying does tend to change your perspective," I said as she shook her head at me. "Am I really dead?"

"You have matured," she said, gazing around us. "Not much, but you have certainly grown since we last spoke. This place is known as Mount Kailash on your plane."

"Mount Kailash? We're in Tibet?"

"Loosely," she replied. "Your body is still in the Keeper's cabin. This immaterial essence"—she pointed at me—"the part that makes you uniquely you, is here with me. Here, we sit nowhere and nowhen."

"That doesn't even begin to make sense."

"Some concepts are beyond you, still."

She was dressed in a loose-fitting, sea-green robe, which was finished with a golden brocade. Indecipherable orange runes flowed around the surface of the robe, and her black hair, pulled into a tight braid, spilled down her back, before coiling onto the floor behind her.

Her blue skin glowed with a not-so-subtle undercurrent of power. She appeared stronger—if that was even possible—than the last time I had seen her.

"You seem stronger," I said. "Is that because I'm dead?"

"Technically, you are not completely dead," she said with a small smile. "The Keeper is doing an admirable job of circumventing my curse; he is quite strong, but my curse is stronger. Currently, you are mostly dead, but that will change soon."

"If I'm mostly dead, does that mean that I'm also slightly alive?"

"It means you will return to your body soon," she said. "Do you know why you are here?"

"I needed to give Monty the catalyst," I said. "In order for that to happen, I needed to die, because the First Elder Rune can't be inside a dead body."

"That is what you have *done*," she said. "I asked you what you were doing *here*—before me, in my place of repose."

"I don't understand. I thought *you* brought me here?"

"Why would I do that?" she asked, cocking her head to one side.

"Because it's *your* curse that keeps me extra alive," I said. "I'm *your* Marked One. I thought if I died, it would be like a reset button with a homing beacon, and bring me back to you."

"A reset button with a homing beacon?"

She gave me a look.

"I mean, I am *your* Aspis, aren't I?"

"Yes," she said. "There is only one living Aspis at any time. You are my chosen, but you do not *belong* to me."

"I don't understand."

"Clearly," she said, staring at me intently. "I will try to simplify it for you."

"Please."

"Do you worship me?"

"I don't, no," I said. "No offense, but my experiences with the divine have shown me that it would be a bad policy to do something like that, with any god or goddess."

"None taken," she answered with a slight smile. "This means you have free will."

"It's not feeling very free these days."

"Regardless of your feelings, you make your own choices, yes?"

"Yes," I said. "I do."

"Since you do not worship, nor pledge direct allegiance to me, why would I lay claim to you upon your death?"

"Because I'm your Marked One?"

*She gave me a look that said, You can't possibly be this dense.*

"You are my Marked One while living because, unlike your predecessors, you do *not* serve me, nor do you wish to."

"You're saying you marked me because I don't want to be marked?" I asked, catching a glimpse of her logic. "How can I be your Marked One and not be one of your worshippers?"

"Blind devotion has its uses," she said. "But it is blind, failing to see where I would prefer clarity of vision and, on occasion, even defiance."

"So you're saying it doesn't make sense that I would come here, to your place of rest when I died?"

"No," she said, staring at me. "Then again, nothing about you makes sense. You should have died the day I cursed you, and yet you didn't."

"About that," I started. "Were you *trying* to kill me?"

She intensified her stare, and I fell into her eyes, floating in the midst of stars being born and dying. Around me, everywhere I looked, was an endless universe—galaxies, clusters, and superclusters filled my vision.

In the midst of all that, I felt atomically small.

"Do you really think I need to *try*?"

Her voice brought me back, and the cold realization that I was sitting in front of the goddess of creation and destruction—heavy on the destruction, in this form—gripped me. Her gaze cut right through me, exposing all of my deepest fears, my darkest thoughts, and my brightest hopes.

Nothing hid me from her infinite gaze.

"No," I said, tearing my eyes away from hers. "Then why curse me alive? Why not strike me down right then and there when I messed up your plan?"

"I have explained this to you. Have you forgotten?"

"I remember; destruction is easy, creation is hard," I said, frustration creeping into my voice against my will. "You cursed me as an expression of creation."

"You have free will?"

"Yes."

"So do I," she said. "Cursing you was *my* choice, with all that implies."

I had never considered that Kali may have *wanted* to curse me alive, despite the fact that I screwed up her five-thousand-year plan against Shiva.

She certainly hadn't had no choice. She could have blasted me to particles.

It was very possible she was looking at this whole situation in a big-picture, long-term kind of way. Anyone—goddess or not—who could follow a plan for five thousand years and not go scorched earth when I blew it to bits knew a thing or two about patience and restraint.

Or, she simply could have wanted to share the pain of making me live long enough to see everyone I knew die. There were enough promises of pain and suffering in her previous threats against me to form that conclusion, too.

It was hard to tell what really motivated a goddess like her.

"Are you saying I'm some kind of strange experiment?" I asked. "You cursed me just to see what would happen?"

"No," she said. "I knew what would happen; and, frankly, in the moment, I was seething with anger. How could one human, full of bravado and bumbling around, undo five thousand years of careful planning and preparation?"

"Monty helped, you know."

"I know," she said. "I wanted to tear you apart and then tear apart the pieces. After that, I wanted to reassemble you and start all over, repeatedly."

It may not have been the wisest move to bring up ruining her plan against Shiva.

"Good thing you don't hold grudges," I said with a small smile, trying to add levity to my voice. "Right?"

"Simon, I am a goddess of destruction," she clarified. "Most of the destruction I unleash is in the form of retribution. When it comes to grudges, I am *the* goddess of grudges—held long and delivered cold to exact great pain and devastation on my targets. I hold grudges long and hard."

I held up a hand in surrender.

"That day you were upset," I said. "Maybe you're still a little upset."

"Yes I was and I am."

"But you didn't kill me."

"Obviously," she said, raising an eyebrow. "since you sit here before me...well, most of you."

"It didn't really make sense to me then, and it barely makes any sense to me now," I said, still feeling slightly confused. "You mark me as your Marked One, and then unleash successors on me."

"Yes." She said the word with a smile that drove a cold spike of fear into my stomach. "It has proven quite illuminating."

I stomped on the fear that rose inside of me and kept going.

"You curse me alive, but when I die, you refuse to claim my...whatever this immaterial essence of mine is, when I appear before you."

"Correct," she said. "Even if I were to attempt to explain it to you, it would be akin to the communication between you and your hellhound."

"I'm not smart enough to figure it out?"

"It has nothing to do with intelligence," she said, waving

my words away. "It has everything to do with deep compre-hension."

"Don't you need one for the other?"

"No," she said. "You are intelligent enough to know that beings of power dwell in and beyond your plane of existence, correct?"

"Yes."

"But lacking the level of power they possess, you do not have the comprehension of the staggering amount of energy you confront on a regular basis," she said, with another slight smile. This one didn't freak me out. "This facilitates your flip-pant responses, born out of fear and ignorance. Your lack of comprehension, though potentially fatal, has allowed you to navigate this new world you find yourself in—at least until now."

"The Keeper," I said. "Gault is a major threat."

"Is he? He is no greater than some of the threats you have faced in the past," she said. "Wouldn't you agree?"

"I would," I said, thinking back to some of the creatures, monsters, and beings Monty and I had faced. "Monty and I have faced some serious threats."

"Then what makes Gault different?"

"This goes back to you and *your* choice, doesn't it?" I asked. "I don't understand why you chose to curse me alive. I try to wrap my head around it, and every time I think I have a handle on it, I come up with a different reason, a different meaning."

"What does it mean to you now" she asked, "when every-thing in your plane hangs on the outcome of the choices you and the mage will make?"

I paused for a moment.

It wasn't like I wasn't feeling the pressure before, but her stating it that way made me realize why this time was different. Gault was threatening those close to me, those who were important to me.

Previously, Monty and I had dealt with psychomegalomaniacs almost as a matter of principle: destroying the world is bad, and we will stop you. That wasn't what was happening with Gault.

He had attacked Haven, endangered Roxanne, incapacitated Ramirez, obliterated the Randy Rump, and had nearly killed Monty and Peaches. He wasn't an abstract threat. He was coming at us, at me, where it mattered most—my family.

He had made a serious error. By attacking those who meant the most to me, he thought we would surrender the First Elder Rune to protect them. He miscalculated. He didn't think we would go in the other direction—use the Elder Rune to stop him from being a threat ever again.

"I have more to protect, more beyond just the plane or the magical community. I have to protect those who are around me, those who are important to me," I said, thinking it through. "I have to protect everyone I can. Especially from people like Gault."

"How will you do that?" she asked. "You are not a mage."

"I don't need to be a mage to protect my family," I said, and then it hit me—I mean, it *really* hit me. Everything everyone had been trying to tell me for so long took a huge windup and smacked me square upside the head. "I'm so much more than *just* a mage."

She gave me a short bow, which I understood somewhere deep in my brain was a big deal. I returned the bow, making it lower than hers, and hopefully expressing the right amount of respect in return.

"Knowing others is wisdom. Knowing yourself is enlightenment," she said. "Now that you understand the limitations of your thoughts, what will you do?"

"I need to get stronger," I said. "How do I do that?"

"My previous instruction to you has not changed: stand in the gap for those near you," she said. "The day is fast approaching when you will have to choose between creation and destruction. Which will you choose, my Marked One?"

"Am I choosing as your Marked One, then?"

"Like the Aspis, there can only be one Marked One at any given time," she said. "You have the rare distinction of being both at once. You can derive power from both mantles, but the choice can only be made from your true self."

"You never said anything about deriving power from the mantles."

"You never asked," she said. "Understand, however that each mantle has its enemies."

"Like the successors?"

"Yes, but you will garner enemies from each."

"Two mantles means twice the amount of enemies," I said. "Is that what you're saying?"

"Yes," she said. "Drawing power from the mantles will attract enemies to you. Do you still wish to learn how?"

I thought about Dira, out there hunting me down and attracting another successor like her. I couldn't even imagine what the enemy of the Aspis would be like. I decided to wait on finding out.

"I'm going to go with no, at least not right now."

"As you wish."

"This choice I have to make—will anyone be able to help me with it?"

"No," she said with a smile. "This will be your choice and your choice alone. Know that although you make this choice alone, it will affect countless lives."

"All because of *my* choice?"

"As you like to say: no pressure."

"I would really like a life of no pressure," I complained.

"That would be excellent. If you could throw in a beach and a hammock, it would be perfect."

"If you had wanted a life devoid of pressure, you should have never thwarted my plan," she said, a trace of anger in her voice. "Choices and actions have consequences. You know this."

"I do."

"Even now, this act you have undertaken will exact a heavy cost—a cost that will have to be paid in order to stop the Keeper."

"Will I be able to pay this cost?"

"That is not the correct question," she said. "Your time here grows to a close. You will return shortly to your body; the Keeper will not be able to suppress my curse much longer."

"What is the correct question?"

"When you understand why you came to me, to my place of repose, you will know the right question."

She extended an arm, palm facing me, and whispered a word under her breath.

"You know, that really doesn't help—"

She waved her fingers down, as if saying goodbye.

Blinding blue light wrapped around me, and the temple disappeared from sight.

# SEVENTEEN

I crashed back into my body to the sounds of growling, groans, and barely controlled mayhem. The glowing violet of the circle I lay in began to slowly fade away.

I took a moment to take in the scene inside the cabin.

Peaches was straining against a golden tether of energy round his neck that connected him to Evergreen. I guessed it was some kind of substitute to the bond we shared.

Evergreen held the tether in his hand and Peaches was pulling in the opposite direction. If it hadn't been so serious, it would have been hilarious.

Evergreen had driven stakes of orange energy into the floor of the cabin, and staked out a large area around the both of them. Peaches would reach the end of the tether and attempt to get past the stakes, only to slam into an invisible wall of energy that flared orange when he hit it, bouncing him back several feet.

Every few seconds, my hellhound would increase in size and attempt to drag Evergreen across the floor, before shrinking back to normal size and trying to slip the tether.

Both strategies were unsuccessful. To his credit, Evergreen didn't budge an inch, but I could see him struggling to keep my now feral hellhound under control.

<RELEASE ME, KEEPER, OR SUFFER DEATH.>

I shook my head at the intensity of my hellhound's voice in my head.

Peaches whirled around and blasted the twin beams of his baleful glare at Evergreen, who raised a hand and deflected them, punching holes into a nearby wall. I looked around and saw that many sections of the walls looked like Swiss cheese.

Peaches squared off against Evergreen and growled as he dug his paws into the stone floor and took a deep breath. He was about to either unleash a bark of massive proportions or else intended to flambé Evergreen where he stood.

"Peaches, no," he warned, holding up a hand and wagging a finger at him. "Do not do this. Simon will be back soon. Just hold on. You are a good hellhound. A good hellhound does not try to bake people."

Judging from the scorch marks around Evergreen, and the singed parts of his clothing, Peaches had tried to barbecue him a few times already. I saw Monty holding a large sphere of white energy in his hands and struggling to keep it inside his circle. His face was drawn and tense as sweat ran profusely down his face.

It did not look good.

The violet circle around me rapidly vanished until I could see clearly. Evergreen locked eyes with me, and a visible expression of relief came over his face. He gestured with his free hand and disappeared the stakes in the ground around them.

"If you would be so kind to re-establish your bond," Evergreen called out as his arm was tugged violently to one side, "I can assist Tristan with the containment cast."

With another gesture, he removed the tether connecting

him to my hellhound. I ran over to my hellhound and wrapped my arms around him. He turned suddenly, about to sink his massive fangs into me. A warm wave of energy overcame me and immediately I felt our deep connection.

*<Hey, boy. I'm back!>*

His eyes came into focus and instead of biting me in half, he slapped me repeatedly with his enormous tongue, pushing me back and causing me to fall onto my back. I saw Evergreen rush over to Monty's circle.

*<You've come back! You've come back!>*

*<I have. I'm not hurt, so you can stop trying to drown me now.>*

*<My saliva will restore you. You were gone. I could not follow.>*

*<I know. I was pretty far away.>*

*<I am your bondmate. You cannot go where I cannot follow.>*

*<I won't.>*

I rubbed his massive head as he nudged further into my chest, placing his giant paws on my legs and pushing forward onto my lap.

*<Whoa, boy. You're not exactly a lap dog, you know.>*

*<I am the Mighty Peaches. I almost hurt the Green Keeper.>*

*<Evergreen?>*

*<Yes. He tried to hold me, but he is not my bondmate. I wanted to attack him, to break free to find you, but he wouldn't let me go.>*

*<Looks like you tried a few times.>*

*<He is very strong—I did not hurt him. But I could not find you, and he would not let go.>*

*<If he had, you would've been lost. I don't think you were going to find me. Even I didn't know where I was.>*

He chuffed and plopped down next to me.

*<I know. You were lost and I could not smell you. I was angry and sad and angry.>*

*<I'm sorry I had to do that. It was the only way to give Monty that power.>*

*<I was sorry too. But now I am happy. Did you bring meat?>*

*<I'm really sorry, boy.>*

*<I smell meat. In your clothes.>*

A sudden weight materialized in my jacket.

Peaches sniffed around me and buried his nose in one of my pockets. I pushed him away and checked the pocket, finding a large sausage. Attached to one end, I saw a small note that read: *This should facilitate what you are looking for. Share this with the Mighty One. —Kali*

I furrowed my brow. *What I'm looking for? Share it with my hellhound?*

My stomach growled as I looked at the sausage. The aroma of the smoked meat hit me, and suddenly I realized I was starving.

Did she really mean I was supposed to eat this sausage *with* him, or just give it to him? I had never shared a sausage with him in that sense. I didn't think that would go over well with my hellhound. I turned the note over and saw more text:

*Yes, half for you and half for him. Then, step back.*

Peaches sniffed the air again.

*<What do you have there? That looks like meat.>*

*<Because it is. I don't know how it got in my pocket.>*

*<Did you make it? If you made it, you can have it.>*

*<You're saying no to meat?>*

*<Only if you made it.>*

Amazing. I was getting insulted by the hellhound version of Gordon Ramsay. He approached the sausage again and sniffed it longer this time.

*<You did not make this meat. This is special meat. Who made this meat?>*

*<It is special. Kali made it for us. We're supposed to share.>*

*<Share? What do you mean, share?>*

I easily tore the large sausage in half.

*<Half for you and half for me?>*

*<Why?>* He eyed both halves. *<You are not a growing hell-hound. You are not a hellhound at all.>*

*<If Kali says we share, we share. Now hurry up—I think Monty needs help.>*

I extended his half, and he begrudgingly took it from my hand. The next moment, he tossed his head up and the sausage disappeared into his bottomless belly.

He growled and rumbled with appreciation.

*<You did not make that meat. That meat was better than the meat from the place. Can we go visit the blue goddess again? This time, maybe she will make meat just for me?>*

I bit into my half, and my mouth exploded with the flavor of the absolute best smoked and honeyed sausage I had ever tasted in my entire life. I ate my half nearly as fast as he ate his. He chuffed in approval.

*<If you keep eating meat like that, one day you will be mighty, like me.>*

*<It was delicious, but I don't understand why she would...?>*

A warm sensation flooded my stomach and I saw the runes on Peaches' flanks blaze with red energy. The mark on my hand burst with white and golden light, and too late I remembered Kali's final instruction: *Then, step back.*

Several things happened at once. My hellhound's head crashed into me, knocking me back as he immediately increased in size. Evergreen turned his head sharply in our direction as red runes appeared on my forearms. They were the similar to the runes my hellhound had along his flanks with a slight variation. My hellhound growled next to me and I noticed it was a much deeper growl than his usual fear-inducing warning of imminent shredding.

He had grown.

He wasn't exactly XL size, but somewhere in between XL and his regular size. The top of his head came up level with my own and his fur went from deep black to black with a metallic sheen.

"What the h—" I started as I looked down at the runes on my arm. "What is happening?"

I turned to look at my hellhound as Evergreen dashed in front of me, extending a hand in my face and deflecting the violet beams that shot out of my eyes. He gestured quickly, and the warm sensation in my stomach went from surface-of-the-sun scorching, to uncontrolled raging inferno.

With another gesture aimed at Peaches, the heat inside my body calmed down almost entirely, only to be replaced with a ravenous hunger.

"Kali's sense of timing leaves much to be desired," Evergreen said, eyeing me suspiciously as he lowered his hand. "Do you feel hungry?"

"I could eat an entire cow right now," I said as my stomach growled. "Why am I so hungry?"

"Come with me," he said, walking toward Monty's circle. "Tristan still needs help, and you may actually be able to help with the process."

"Help? How?"

"No questions—I need you to do as instructed," he said, his voice grim. "Can you do that? I promise to answer all your questions afterward if there is an afterward."

The tone of his voice made me focus. Whatever Monty was dealing with, the containment cast wasn't going as planned.

"Do not step into his circle," Evergreen warned as we approached Monty. "When I tell you, fire those beams of yours into that sphere of energy he is holding."

"I'll hit Monty," I said. "I don't want to hit him."

"Aim, and make sure you don't," Evergreen snapped. "I can't output enough energy in my current state. Not after dealing with your hellhound trying to rip, bark, and bake me into oblivion. I'm on my last legs as it is."

I heard the verge of panic in the fringes of his voice.

"What do you need me to do exactly?"

"Stand over there, parallel to Tristan," he said, pointing. "That way if your aim is off, you won't inadvertently hit him."

"Then what?"

"You blast those beams of yours into that sphere," he said. "Only the beams, nothing else. Your life force cannot be part of this equation. Do not cast your missile or anything else that draws from your life force. Understood?"

"I barely know how I unleashed those beams the first time," I said. "I don't know if I can do that again."

"You can. Trust me," he said. "When I remove the limiter I've placed on you both, fire your beams at the sphere and only the sphere."

"Do you want Peaches to fire his as well?"

"No!" he said quickly. "No. We need a source of power that won't obliterate everything. Please make sure he does not use his baleful glare."

*<Hey, boy.>*

*<Yes, bondmate. I heard, and the Keeper is correct in his assessment. My baleful glare would obliterate the cabin, the mage, the Keeper, and the very plane we stand in, were I to unleash the power contained within it. Your glare is still weak; it will prove adequate.>*

*<Thanks?>*

*<You are welcome. You must focus. Once he removes the limiter, the power will try to overwhelm you. You must maintain control.>*

*<I'm so hungry. I could do with Ezra's pastrami sandwich right now. Maybe two of them.>*

*<Perhaps after we leave this plane, we can procure vast amounts of meat. For now, you should prepare. The Keeper is going to remove the limiter.>*

"Are you ready?" Evergreen asked.

"Not really, but we don't have much of a choice," I said. "Do it."

Evergreen, who was sweating almost as much as Monty by now, traced several symbols in the air around us. Immediately, the uncontrolled raging inferno ratcheted up to supernova, as heat flowed out from my midsection to fill my entire body.

Power flowed through me and I felt as if I would burst. A flood of information assaulted my brain—smells, sounds, and sensations I had never experienced before overloaded me. I nearly collapsed, but my hellhound stood behind me, supporting me with his head.

*<His plan is flawed, bondmate. If you blast that sphere with your glare, the mage will die.>*

*<What? I don't want to kill Monty.>*

*<There is an alternative.>*

*<What alternative?>*

*<Your blade. Siphon the excess energy of the First Elder Rune without taking it into your body. Allow the mage to contain it slowly within himself and he will possess the entire First Elder Rune without suffering harm.>*

*<Are you sure that will work? How do you know this? You aren't a mage.>*

*<Neither are you. Fortunately for the mage, we are so much more. Trust me. My knowledge, my true knowledge, stems from the blood in my veins, which is older than this Keeper or the First Elder Rune. I know of what I speak. Enter the circle.>*

He nudged me forward with his massive head.

I stepped forward and Evergreen grabbed me by the arm. He pulled it away immediately with a hiss, looking down at his burned palm.

I glanced at him and shook my head.

"You can't go in that circle," he warned. "It will kill Tristan."

"Your solution is flawed," I said. "Feeding more power into the sphere will only cause a catastrophic cascade. Monty cannot contain the rune like that. What he needs is a siphon."

"How would you even know that?" Evergreen demanded. "Only a—"

I raised a finger and pointed at Peaches.

"He saw the fundamental flaw, and if he knows it, I know it," I said. "Now stand back. We have this."

Evergreen resisted and stood his ground, blocking my path for a few seconds, until Peaches growled. He moved then and stood back. His face was a mixture of grim determination and surprise.

I stepped up to the white circle and gazed at Monty.

Even though he was fighting with the containment cast, he was still aware of everything that was occurring around him.

"Good to see you could make it back," he said, his voice strained. "It seems this cast was too much for me."

"Looks that way. I can help you, but you have to let go of the cast."

"Let go of the cast?" he asked incredulously. "It will spiral out of control if I do that."

"Tristan, you can't," Evergreen called out from behind me. "His mind must be affected by his recent death. If you let go of that cast, it will kill us all."

Evergreen took a step toward Monty, and Peaches growled behind me. Evergreen decided that remaining in one piece was a great idea. I glanced at him, and then turned all my attention to Monty.

"Do you trust me?" I asked him. "I know I don't do finger-wiggles like you, but this—I know this will work."

"I trust you unequivocally," he said, his voice strained further. "You know that."

"Let go," I said as I formed Ebonsoul and stepped into the circle. "Now."

Monty extended his arms to his sides and let go of the sphere.

White light exploded into the cabin as the cast broke through the containment sphere and flooded the room with energy.

# EIGHTEEN

"Give me your hand," I said, extending my arm to Monty. "When I begin siphoning, you begin containing the energy inside of you."

He nodded and gripped my hand tight.

I plunged Ebonsoul into the cloud of energy that hovered in front of us. This wasn't just the catalyst—this was the entire First Elder Rune.

Ebonsoul thrummed with power as it siphoned the energy into itself. The cloud of white energy began to twist around us in a whirlwind of power and, slowly, it funneled into Ebonsoul.

Within, I blocked the siphoned energy and allowed it to flow outward to Monty. The white cloud flowed into his arm as he whispered under his breath and gestured with his other hand. After what felt like hours, but was probably closer to minutes, the energy cloud in front of us was gone.

Monty held the entire First Elder Rune within him.

I saw no outward indicator of the rune until he looked at me. The golden rings that circled his irises had increased in intensity. They now fluctuated between gold and white, giving his eyes a weird strobe effect.

"It's going to be a little hard to hide that," I said, pointing at his eyes. "I'm sure Zegna makes some killer sunglasses or contacts. Either that, or you can be the mage that's all the rage at every rave."

He looked at me as if I had lost my mind. My laugh at the end of my comment probably didn't convince him of my sanity at the moment. I was feeling a little off. Even though I hadn't absorbed the power of the elder rune, its presence in my body, even temporarily, still had after effects.

"What are you talking about?"

"You'll see," I said as the white circle we stood in disappeared. I turned to face an awestruck Evergreen, who stood looking at us with his mouth open. "Done."

I took a few steps out of the circle, and was wondering why the cabin had turned ninety degrees. I was about to ask Monty about the rotation when I managed to introduce my face to the cabin floor, as a burst of white light and runes filled my vision.

"Welcome back," Monty said, looking down at me. "Hungry?"

"I was starving earlier. Now, not so much," I said and attempted to sit up. The room decided this was the perfect moment to start spinning and began rotating. I closed my eyes until it settled down. "Why don't I feel like I want to devour a herd of cattle?"

"It appears that during his battle form, you are linked symbiotically with your hellhound," he said, glancing over to where my now normal-sized hellhound was destroying an enormous bowl of pastrami. Around the bowl he was eliminating, I saw three others that were empty. "I think he's finally satiated."

Peaches moved away from the bowl, crossed over near to

where I lay, and collapsed to the floor with a loud *thump*. Seconds later, he was snoring.

"What just happened?" I asked, looking from Monty to Evergreen. "Explain in small words please. You said something about a battle form?"

Evergreen just shook his head. Monty pulled up a chair and sat closer.

"You recall learning that your hellhound has a battle form, yes?" he asked. "A state that would make you two a formidable force to be reckoned with."

"Yes, I remember," I said. "Is that what happened?"

"Not entirely," Monty said, glancing at my hellhound. "Somehow the combination of your demise and that sausage you ate with him triggered a battle form state. Evergreen informs me it wasn't a true battle form, but closer to a practice run."

"Kali spiked the sausage," I said, remembering the sausage. "She said it contained what I was looking for."

"Technically, she was correct," he said, "though her sense of timing could have been better. She had to have known you would've fed that sausage to your hellhound immediately upon its discovery."

"I was not looking for a battle form of any kind."

"You were looking for a deeper connection with your hellhound," he said. "I can't imagine a deeper connection than a battle form. It transcends your normal bond by orders of magnitude. In essence, you almost become one entity."

I remembered how I had communicated with Peaches. It felt as if we had shared one mind. We were more than connected—we *were* one.

"I can understand that."

"What made you eat half of the sausage?" he asked. "You never share food with your hound."

"I know, but it smelled so good and I was hungry."

"I see," he said, pensively. "That may be a component of the symbiosis. I think the Keeper has more answers for you. Evergreen?"

Evergreen cleared his throat and removed a book from one of the bookshelves.

"The information on hellhounds and their bondmates is ancient, predating even me," he said. "It's scarce and difficult to decipher, but what I *can* tell you is that the battle form of a hellhound and its bondmate has several phases: from the lowest phase, which it appears you nearly experienced today, to the highest, which I have never seen but only read about."

"Who would know more about this?" I asked. "I think it would be important to understand how this happened. The last thing I need is to be walking down the street with my hellhound and shift into this *terrorize the city* battle form."

"I would imagine Hades would have more information for you," Monty said. "We can ask him if we survive Gault."

"The First Elder Rune," I said suddenly, looking at him closely. "Are you okay?"

"So far," he said, looking off to the side before closing his eyes. "I can't hold it indefinitely. The containment is holding, thanks to your siphon."

"I must express my deepest apologies," Evergreen said and gave us a short bow. "You were chosen because you presented the best chance of success against Gault, and when it mattered most, I doubted you."

"No apologies needed," I said. "I would've doubted me, too."

Evergreen looked out of the window before turning back to us.

"We need to go, don't we?" I continued. "How long have we been gone?"

"On your plane, you've been missing for close to an hour,"

Evergreen answered. "I only regret that I cannot join you when you face Gault."

"You can't," Monty said. "If he kills you, he can take control of the First Elder Rune."

"We can't let that happen," I said. "Monty, can you control the First Elder Rune?"

"To a degree," he said. "If we're going to face Gault, we're going to need help."

"I thought we couldn't call anyone to help us?"

"We can't call anyone who doesn't possess the First Elder Rune for help," he said. "But there is someone who can face him and survive. Someone who possesses part of Gault's own rune inside her body."

"Lotus," I said when the realization hit. "Will she help us?"

"Let's go find out," Monty said, getting to his feet. "How do you feel?"

"Getting better by the second," I said, getting out of the futon. My body felt completely restored, and an undercurrent of energy coursed through me. "Actually, I'm feeling much better."

"You recall the activation sequence?" Evergreen asked, looking at Monty. "At most you will have two, maybe three casts before the rune destroys the containment cast. If you still possess it when that happens—"

"It will be the last time I cast, ever."

Evergreen nodded.

"It will obliterate you," Evergreen said. "No siphon will save you then. Do not let it come to that. Deal with Gault and preserve your life."

"That is the whole of my intention," Monty said. "Can you open a portal to the interstice?"

"Yes," Evergreen said, extending a hand. "I hope this is not the last time we all see one another. We still have so much to learn and there are many conversations we still need to have."

Monty took his hand and shook it firmly. I did the same, and my hellhound padded over and nudged Evergreen with his head.

"No hard feelings," Evergreen said, rubbing Peaches' over-sized head. "I know now that you only acted in the best interests of your bondmate and his bond brother."

Peaches chuffed at him and then came over to stand by my side.

"Remember why you fight," Evergreen said. "Remember who you fight for."

"We will," Monty said as I nodded. "Thank you."

Evergreen gestured and formed a portal.

# NINETEEN

We stepped through the portal and found ourselves in a large, green, open field.

"This looks like Dex's—"

"Yes," Monty said, waving a hand in front of him. A small house appeared in front of us. "This interstice is connected to my uncle's room in the Moscow."

Lotus stepped out of the house and waited for us by the entrance. I noticed something was missing.

"Monty? Where are her cuffs?"

"I removed them," he said. "There was no need for them any longer. Not in here."

"Why not?" I asked warily. "She's still a servant of Gault. She has a part of his rune in her. Did you forget that symbol on her chest? You know, the one that can undo everything around her? The entropic absolution—you don't remember?"

"Entropic dissolution," Monty corrected. "That one?"

"Yes, that one," I said. "What were you thinking?"

"I was thinking that Lotus had been held against her will for long enough," Monty answered. "She deserved her freedom."

"Even if she dissolves everything?"

"Not everything," Lotus said, staring at me. "If I had wished you harm, I would have never entered this space willingly."

"You were cuffed when Monty brought you here," I said. "You didn't have a choice."

"True, but the inhibitors were only so effective against me," she said, producing the rune-covered cuffs and tossing them to the ground next to her. "I have other skills that do not rely on being a mage. Just because I'm a mage doesn't mean that I'm not *more* than a mage."

"How did you—?" I said, looking at the cuffs. "They didn't work on you?"

"Before Gault forced me to serve him, I had to survive by my wits and skills," she said, her voice becoming serious. "I couldn't depend on my magic to solve everything, so I became adept at using my gift to see opportunities. Inhibitors work on mages; I just found a way around them."

"She can use her gift to see the flaws in the cuffs and exploit them using physical means," Monty said. "It's quite clever."

"You have the First Elder Rune," she said, looking at Monty. "Honestly, I didn't think you could do it. That is a Keeper's rune. Even now I can see you're just barely holding on."

"Just barely," Monty said with a nod. "Are you prepared? Facing Gault will be a challenge."

"A challenge?" I said. "He nearly killed you last time. Nearly killed us."

"I'm with Simon on this one," Lotus said as Peaches rumbled in her direction. "Facing Gault on our own is suicide."

"We can't ask anyone else," Monty said. "We either stop

him or give him the First Elder Rune. There is no middle ground."

"We can't give him the rune," she said. "He's insane. He'll kill everyone to create his perfect society. We can't let him."

Peaches rumbled again and padded over to Lotus, sniffing the air and circling around her, before coming to sit in front of her and rumbling again.

"Strong, what is your hellhound doing?" Lotus asked nervously. "Did I offend him or something?"

I raised a finger in response.

"One second."

*<What is it, boy?>*

*<She still smells bad, but it's not her smell. The badness belongs to the other Keeper, the one who hurt the angry man.>*

*<Gault. He's the one we have to stop.>*

*<He put badness in her, to hurt her. We have to help her.>*

*<She's going to help us stop Gault.>*

*<Good. She can help us, and then the angry man can take out the badness.>*

*<I don't know if Monty can.>*

*<If he doesn't, she will get sick. The badness will take over.>*

*<We'll do what we can.>*

*<My saliva can't help her. Not with this.>*

*<I understand. Let me tell them.>*

I explained my hellhound's prognosis and Lotus nodded.

"He's quite perceptive," she said, looking down at Peaches. "Only a Keeper can remove this mark. I doubt Gault will cooperate with my request."

"Even if you ask him politely?"

She gave me a sad smile.

"Especially if I ask him politely," she answered. "My only hope of getting rid of this *badness,* as your hellhound calls it, is to stop Gault once and for all."

"We have the tools," Monty said, "but nothing is guaranteed. We will strive to the utmost to do above and beyond our best. With determination and some luck, we will prevail over this evil. Or die trying."

I gave Monty a short golf clap before tapping him on the shoulder.

"That was actually uplifting," I said. "Really, I have chills. For a mage speech, it was absolutely horrible—not enough doom and gloom, except for that bit at the end—but overall, your morale-building pep talks are getting much better."

Lotus just stared at us.

"Right," Monty said, pulling on his jacket. "Lotus and I will confront Gault initially; Simon, you will hang back and deal with the Darkanists until I give you the signal to join in the fray."

"I'm dealing with the Darkanists alone?" I asked, surprised. "I mean, yes, I'm awesome, I just don't think I'm *that* level of awesome."

"You forgot the ogres, trollgres, and thralls," Monty said. "I'm certain he will have plenty of those to throw at us."

"I take back what I said about your morale building getting better," I answered with a dark expression. "I can't handle all of that alone, not even with my mighty hellhound. We'll be overrun in seconds."

"You will have some assistance," he said, still not filling me with any confidence. "Your job is to keep them away from Lotus and me. Gault will use them as cannon fodder in his attempt to bog us down and have unfettered access to the First Elder Rune. You won't let him."

"Are you sure you two can face him...alone?" I asked. "Isn't that giving him what he wants? Unfettered access?"

"We're not completely alone," Monty said, resting a hand on my shoulder. "We'll get his attention, and together we'll put an end to his madness."

"And to him," Lotus said, her words hard and final. "We put an end to him."

Monty nodded and gestured, forming a large, green circle.

"Once we leave the interstice, Gault will know we have the Lotus and the First Elder Rune," Monty said. "He will send his minions at us in force."

"I'm sure he'll be eager to say hello in the most violent way possible," I said. "We need a place that won't create collateral damage."

"That circle will take us to Little Island off Pier 54," Monty clarified. "Specifically, near the amphitheater situated in the northwest corner of the island."

"It will be packed with people," I said. "That place is popular."

"Not with the aversion runes placed around the Pier," Monty said. "They should last for at least another four hours. I don't foresee a protracted battle with Gault. Either we meet and present a credible threat, or he destroys us immediately. Neither option will take four hours."

"Now I'm full of confidence, thanks," I said. "Wait, this place is an actual island? How many points of ingress?"

"Two," Monty said. "Pier 54 has a short footbridge which leads to the east end of the island. Another unnamed, and longer footbridge sitting over what used to be Pier 55 leads to the north end."

I gave the situation some thought.

The moment we arrived on Little Island, we were going to be swarmed by Gault's creatures and Darkanists. I figured the Darkanists could port in some of the creatures, but not all of them. The bulk of the minion army would have to use the footbridges.

"We need to Battle of Thermopylae this thing," I said. "We destroy the shorter footbridge and force them to take the longer one to reach us."

"The longer footbridge will force them to make a right angle to reach the island," Monty said. "You can make your stand there."

"You had this place prepped, didn't you?" I asked. "There's no way you've just now scoped this place out."

He nodded.

"Forewarned is forearmed," he said. "I have scouted several locations throughout the city for occasions such as this. Little Island is the ideal location to confront Gault and his forces."

"You have locations prepped for last stands? Really?"

"Yes, really," he said. "I'm a mage. This is what we do in our free time—think of places to confront death."

"You really need to get a hobby," I said, shaking my head. "Something that doesn't involve death."

"Duly noted," he replied. "Some of Gault's forces will be teleported in by the Darkanists. Since you will be on the footbridge initially, you need to be wary of a deadly flanking maneuver. Your assistance should help in that regard."

"About my assistance," I said. "They can't confront Gault directly, but they can kick ogres, Darkanists, and thralls into the beyond?"

"Yes. I'm certain you will approve," he said, and began to gesture. "Let's not keep Gault waiting."

Lotus nodded.

"It's time," she said. "Let's finish this."

# TWENTY

We arrived on Little Island in the middle of a green field with a winding, stone path cutting right through the center.

As far as little islands went, Scola Isle was much smaller, but I understood the idea behind the construction of this place. Unlike Scola, this entire island was a park that sat on platforms resembling large concrete tulips, just off the west edge of Manhattan.

The amphitheater was behind us, and off in the distance I saw the footbridges. The island wasn't as small as Scola, but it wasn't enormous either, being roughly the size of two football fields.

As a field of battle though? The square island was cramped and small, but the size also meant we could control the flow of the fighting. Monty raised a hand and formed a bright white orb the size of a basketball.

Then after he whispered a word I didn't understand, and it began to rotate.

It hovered above his hand for a few seconds before racing off in the direction of the short concrete footbridge on Pier

54. It descended as it approached, and then smashed into the footbridge, reducing it to dust.

"One conventional way in and one conventional way off the island now," Monty said. "Though I'm certain Gault will be anything but conventional."

"How soon before Gault heads this way?" I asked, looking east to where the city was. "He must sense you by now, right?"

Monty slashed the air next to him, creating two portals. Through one, I saw the amphitheater that sat behind us on the edge of the island. For a second, it threw me, since I was seeing the theater both in the distance and close up through the portal.

The second portal led to the remaining footbridge, where I would keep Gault's forces occupied. I looked through the portal and noticed the absence of any other people or artillery standing near the footbridge.

"Monty?" I asked, still looking through the portal and pointing. "I'm noticing the space near the footbridge is pretty empty. This assistance you mentioned before, are they invisible? Tell me they're invisible."

"They will be there," he said as he looked up into the sky. "Remember: slow them down. They will press you to get to us. You only have to slow them down enough to allow us to create an opening."

"An opening?" I asked, not entirely understanding this plan. "An opening for who?"

"For me," Monty said. "I only have, at most, three opportunities to stop Gault with the First Elder Rune."

"Then I should be there next to you," I said, realizing he and Lotus were going to face Gault on their own. "I can help create an opening, especially with my mighty hellhound."

He shook his head.

"Why do you think you're slowing down the forces and

not facing Gault directly?" Monty asked. "Only those who have the First Elder Rune or Gault's own rune can stand against him."

"I can definitely... Oh, hell."

"You no longer carry the catalyst," Lotus said. "You have no defenses against his power now. If you face him directly, he *will* kill you."

"That's easier said than done," I said. "I can still—"

"You will. Just not in the initial encounter," Monty said. "I'd rather not have you die repeatedly in an effort to wear him down. Your energy would be better utilized at the footbridge."

I had to admit he was right. I had totally overlooked the fact that without the catalyst, Gault would shred me before I knew what was happening.

"Won't he think I have the catalyst?" I asked. "I mean, after our last beat-down, won't he still think I have the catalyst and come after me first?"

"No," Monty said, moving to the portal. "He will sense that I have the entire rune and come for it." He glanced at Lotus. "He can also sense her. We need to go."

They stepped into the portal and vanished from sight. I turned to my portal and stepped in with my hellhound by my side. The island compressed and then snapped back to normal.

I arrived at the end of the remaining footbridge and waited. The empty park seemed strange in the middle of the day.

I looked down the footbridge; it was straight for close to thirty feet, then made a hard right and ended sixty feet later on Manhattan.

My hellhound nudged my leg.

<*I smell them.*>

I sniffed the air, but only smelled the Hudson River

around us, which wasn't exactly the healthiest aroma to inhale. I looked around and realized that aside from my hellhound, I was completely alone.

*<Monty said we would have help, but it looks like it's just us.>*

*<I am mighty and you are my bondmate. Together, we are very strong.>*

I rubbed his gigantic head as I heard the distant rumble.

*<They're coming, boy. Don't let the creepy, mangled ones bite or scratch you. Those are the thralls and they're poisonous. Everything else, you can shred.>*

He rumbled as he stood next to me.

I felt a surge of energy behind us and turned as a massive, gauntleted hand touched my shoulder. I formed Ebonsoul and drew Grim Whisper in a smooth motion as I whirled and ducked away from the hand, bringing both my weapons to bear.

"I told you he was ready," Nan said, looking at Braun with a huge grin. "The mage said you would need help. Today, we are here as the shaft of the spear. More of the Midnight Echelon are on their way, though I doubt much will be left for them to do by the time they arrive—Braun is in a foul mood."

"I am not in a foul mood," Braun corrected with a growl. "I just haven't hit anything in some time."

"We just left Haven not an hour ago," Nan said. "You hit plenty there."

"Not enough," Braun said, putting her hands together and cracking her knuckles. "Not nearly enough."

I let go of the breath I had been holding as relief flooded my body. The odds were still stacked against us, but I had two of the Midnight Echelon standing next to me.

We had a chance.

"I'm really glad to see you two," I said. "I don't know how many are headed our way, but we need to stop them here."

"An army is headed our way," Nan said. "Mages, ogres, and even a trollgre or two. The force we faced at Haven was a distraction. The Keeper amassed a much larger force not far from here, at your abode."

"The Moscow?"

"Yes," she said. "I think he has been waiting for you. He did not seem pleased."

"I bet. Did he damage—?"

"The building is protected," Nan said, cutting me off. "Walls of ice worthy of Skadi surround your home. The Keeper tried and failed to enter the building."

"No way little Cece could cover the building with that much ice," I said. "She's still learning how to use her abilities."

"No, it was the other ice mage—though I doubt she is entirely human," Nan said, shaking her head. "The one you call Olga. She is a fearsome warrior, worthy of joining our ranks."

"Olga fought off Gault?"

"You doubt it?" Nan asked. "I saw her freeze and shatter an ogre to pieces with my own eyes. She is strong."

"And prudent," Braun said. "When she saw the bulk of the Keeper's forces approaching, she retreated."

"Yes," Nan said with a nod. "She created the defenses and withstood the onslaught of Gault's creatures."

"They were preparing for another assault when we sensed the mage arrive," Braun said. "The Keeper must have felt the power of the rune. He commanded his army to attack this place."

"Did you see any thralls?" I asked. "They were part of the attacking force at Haven."

Braun spit to the side in disgust.

"Aye, those misshapen creatures cover the streets like

ants," Braun said. "More than several hundred of them advance on us as we speak."

She smiled as she looked off into the direction of the approaching forces.

"Thralls are dangerous," I warned. "They're poisonous. Don't let them wound or bite you."

Braun laughed at my warning.

"Unless it's poison from Jormungandr himself, it will do nothing to us," she said, clapping me on the shoulder and staring into my eyes. "I dare say it should be nothing for you and the Mighty One as well." She looked over at Nan. "They have found their battle form."

"Truly?" Nan asked, hefting her axe onto her shoulder. "Have you mastered it yet?"

"It only happened once, and it was by accident," I explained quickly. "I wouldn't say I've mastered anything."

She nodded.

"The Mighty One will guide you, then," Nan said. "Follow your hellhound and your bond. Listen to his sage counsel; he will guide you true."

"I wish I felt as confident as you sound."

"This is not the battle," she said, looking behind us to where the amphitheater was. "Over there is where the final battle will be fought. We are to hold them until the old one gives us the sign."

"The old one?"

"Once we get the sign, you will join the mage," Nan said. "There, you will join the battle and stop this Keeper."

"I will?" I asked. "Monty said I needed to fight here, until he created an opening."

"And so you shall," Braun said. "Once the opening is created, you and the Mighty One will become the tip of the spear."

"I don't—"

"It will become clear," Nan said with a smile, swinging her hammer by her side. "For now, we fight."

I glanced behind us as the first ogre crashed onto the concrete footbridge. He roared when he saw us and lumbered across, faster than he had any right to move.

Peaches growled and entered maim-and-obliterate mode. He crouched low and growled again, pushing off his hind legs and launching himself forward directly at the approaching ogre.

<With me, bondmate!>

I let my fear and rage mix with the feeling of certain death that filled my body, and screamed as I chased after my hellhound. Nan and Braun were right behind me, laughing as we crossed the footbridge.

"Aye, Strong!" Nan yelled. "*That* is a battlecry."

The air became charged with power as a flash of blue light crossed the sky and descended behind us, followed by a thunder clap that boomed across the island.

We skidded to a stop, as did the ogre.

"The Keeper has arrived," Nan said, then turned back to the ogre. "Your battle cry has improved, Strong. We stop these here for as long as possible. Reduce their numbers and make them bleed for every inch."

She raced forward as Peaches blinked out, and I followed them, with Braun behind me.

# TWENTY-ONE

Nan crashed into the ogre axe-first, removing one of its arms as she rotated, and finished her attack by removing its head. She didn't even slow down as she jumped at the second ogre, shoving him to one side where Braun waited with a fist.

Braun hit the ogre several times, breaking its bones every time her fist connected. By the time she was done, the ogre lay broken on the ground. Her last fist crushed its head, ending its life.

I saw more ogres making their way to the footbridge.

*Where are they all coming from?*

Nan was sweeping them off the bridge with her axe and into the river on either side. Surprisingly, they didn't drown—that would have been too easy, and there was no way we could be that lucky. They jumped out of the river and landed either on the footbridge, on thralls—crushing them in the process—or on the island itself. Behind the ogres, I saw the much larger trollgres: three of them.

The one in the center was familiar. It was hard to forget a face that ugly. He saw me from a distance and roared, pointing in my direction. A wave of thralls appeared behind the trollgre and advanced on us.

I felt, more than saw, my hellhound blink around the footbridge and take out the thralls. A group would be obliterated by one of his barks, and he would be gone before another group could fall on him.

Omega beams cut through another advancing throng, and then he was gone again, never in one place long enough for them to swarm my hellhound.

I fired Grim Whisper, dusting several thralls as the ogres advanced on my position. Braun slid in front of me and punched a hole through one of the approaching ogres before turning to me.

"We each take a trollgre," she called out over the fighting. "That one is the leader. He wants you and has called you out."

"Tell him he has the wrong number."

She was pointing at the trollgre from Haven—if there was a leader to this army of creatures, it was that one.

She laughed as she backhanded an ogre off the footbridge and into the river, while squeezing a thrall with her other hand and tossing its lifeless body to the side.

"You are fighting with the Nightwing, Strong," she said, "an honor bestowed upon few. You can do this. Believe that you can."

"I'm flattered, really," I said, firing Grim Whisper several more times and dropping a few advancing thralls. "I believe *that* trollgre can flatten me in two seconds. That's what *I* believe."

"There is no reward without risk," she said with another laugh as she dodged an ogre's hammer, grabbed its arm, and wrenched it sideways, stripping its weapon before swinging it into the ogre. "See? Easy!"

I just stared at her in awe for a few seconds as I tried to

process what she was asking me to do. She pushed me back as more ogres came at her.

The ogres screamed in rage at her. She gave one an uppercut in response, kicked another in the chest, and shattered the knees of a third, all as she grinned.

"Show it who you are!" she yelled over the roars and screams of violence. "Show them what it means to face the Marked of Kali!"

"You have got to be kidding!" I yelled back as I fired my weapon a few more times, and dropping more thralls around me. "I can't go fight that thing!"

"You don't have to worry about that," Braun answered with a wide smile. "He's coming for you. Prepare!"

She was right. The trollgre was shoving thralls and ogres out of its way and headed for me. I moved back away from the footbridge to where I would have room to maneuver.

I quickly scanned the footbridge and saw Nan engaged with the other trollgre. Braun had made her way to her trollgre, and the leader was closing on me. My hellhound was tearing through the thralls without being touched, but something was still off.

*Where are the Darkanists?*

I holstered Grim Whisper as the trollgre approached. I remembered that this was the trollgre that had punched a crater into a rune-inscribed wall; entropy rounds wouldn't do anything except piss it off.

"Strong," it said as it grinned, turning my stomach in the process. "Kill you."

"I remember you," I said. "How could I forget such a handsome face?"

It roared in response.

I moved back and formed Ebonsoul. Black mist flowed from my hand and formed my blade. The runes along its length glowed white, which they hadn't done in the past.

*That's new.*

The trollgre closed on me and swung a massive fist in an attempt to remove my head. I backpedaled as it lunged forward, leading with its other hand in a grab.

It was fast—faster than anything that size had a right to be.

I jumped back, barely dodging the grab as it rolled forward and barreled into me, knocking the air out of my lungs and Ebonsoul from my hand.

"What the hell?" I managed with a gasp as a punch glanced off my side, while I rolled away from the fist that had left a large crater in the floor. "Since when?"

My curse flared hot, hotter than it ever had.

I managed to get to my feet just as a foot-shaped sledge-hammer kicked me in the side and launched me forward. The trollgre roared again and advanced on me.

This was no ordinary trollgre. It was putting attacks together with a cohesive strategy. I scrambled to my feet, gritting my teeth against the pain, and narrowly dodged another fist designed to crush my chest.

Extending my arm, I formed Ebonsoul again. The white runes along its length blazed with power. I didn't know what it meant, but I had no time to try and figure it out.

The trollgre grinned again and ran at me in a football tackle, arms spread wide. I slid to the side, and it adjusted, still coming for me. It was too fast to avoid, so I did the last thing it expected.

I ran toward the trollgre.

For a split second, my change in tactics confused it—then it roared again and advanced. A split second was all I needed. I slid forward under its arms as it tried to crush me in a lethal bear-hug, and buried Ebonsoul in its chest to the hilt.

It turned to face me as rage covered its face. I was about

to extend my hand and absorb Ebonsoul when the blade exploded with white light, filling the trollgre and forcing me to look away briefly. The trollgre looked down, confused, and clawed at Ebonsoul, trying to remove it.

The next moment, the white energy that had filled the trollgre shifted to black and violet as cracks appeared in its skin. Runes and symbols flowed around it, and as it looked at me with fear and rage in its eyes, the cracks grew ever wider.

As the trollgre fell to its knees, it roared again.

This time, the roar was filled with the pain of a dying creature. I knew deep inside that it was being undone. The energy became golden and grew bright; I had to turn my face from the light as the trollgre roared one last time and then disappeared.

All around me, the fighting continued, but I stood in a pocket of silence. The golden energy that flowed from Ebonsoul coalesced and entered me.

*What the hell was that?*

*The catalyst of the First Elder Rune.*

*Impossible. And I thought I told you I wasn't interested in becoming your puppet?*

*I am not making an offer— I am merely offering information. Your blade still possesses part of the catalyst.*

*How? The entire rune was transferred to Monty.*

*Not entirely. A remnant of the rune bonded to the blade. I do not know how—you are not a Keeper. Perhaps during the transmission of the catalyst, some aspect merged with the blade which forms part of who you are, but this is all conjecture. I am not certain.*

*Doesn't matter what it is right now. I have to focus on staying alive.*

*An excellent strategy, one I highly endorse.*

*Shut it and keep it shut unless I speak to you. Understand?*

*Understood.*

Izanami became silent, and that was when I sensed them.

The Darkanists.

They were creating portals on the island all around us, allowing more ogres and thralls to surround us. The Darkanists had never crossed over to Little Island.

They had remained on Manhattan and were casting from there. There weren't many of them, but I saw a handful creating the portals for the creatures. I reached out for my hellhound.

*<There are mages on the shore opening portals. Stop them.>*

*<Can I bite them?>*

*<Bite them, but don't kill them. Just stop them from casting.>*

*<I can bite and stop them.>*

*<Good, do that. I'll see what I can do here.>*

A massive arm scooped me off my feet and tossed me to the side as Braun deflected an ogre's hammer from crushing my skull.

I rolled to my feet with Ebonsoul in my hand, turning in time to see Braun turn and rip the hammer from the ogre's hand. She slammed it into its chest a few times until it collapsed and lay still. Then she gave it a swift kick and launched it off the island.

"You dispatch one trollgre and stand there dreaming of victory?" Braun asked, still grinning. "There are more enemies to fight, Strong."

"Thanks," I said, moving back to the main force which had gained a foothold on the island just beyond the footbridge. I pointed to the shore. "We need to get those mages—"

A shadow crossed over the spot where I was standing, and then veered off to the shore. The screams started then, and I saw the Darkanists fall. A figure on the shore was wielding an immense hammer and smacking the Darkanists into the next life.

Those who witnessed the attack were the ones screaming as they tried to retaliate. It was a mistake—Maul threw her hammer at the attacking mages, breaking arms and legs as she proceeded to advance on them.

Above us, another valkyrie circled and landed in the middle of several ogres. A few seconds later, she stood alone, gleaming sword in hand.

"You were saying?" Braun asked. "The Nightwing is here, which means you need to go soon."

"Go? Where am I supposed to go?"

She pointed toward the amphitheater.

"You need to become the tip of the spear now," she said, her voice serious. "We will hold them here. You need to go help the mage. End this."

Vi walked up next to me and placed a hand across her chest. I returned the gesture, though I felt strange doing it.

"The old one sends word," she said. "Well met, Strong. Thank you for leaving some for us."

I shook my head. Something was seriously off with these valkyries.

"What old one?" I asked. "Who sent word?"

"You know him as Dexter," Vi said.

"Dexter is the old one?" I asked. "How?"

"No time to explain," she said, glancing at Braun. "Phase two has started."

She pointed and I saw a green beam shoot down into the amphitheater.

"Summon your hound, Strong. Your part in this battle here is over," she said and tore open a portal with her blade. "You must go now."

I was about to call Peaches when he appeared next to me with a loud rumble.

*<I'm ready.>*

*<How did you...? I didn't even call you.>*

*<You did. We must go.>*

Vi pointed to the portal.

"We will speak if we are still standing after this," she continued. "Go."

We stepped through the portal.

# TWENTY-TWO

We ended up at the edge of the amphitheater.

We were surrounded by Darkanists who screamed when Peaches and I stepped out of the portal. Some of them recovered more quickly than others, forming orbs to unleash at us.

They were fast—they just weren't faster than my hellhound.

Peaches blinked in and out repeatedly. Every time he reappeared, he'd take down another Darkanist. The bulk of their force was here, supporting and dying for Gault.

Peaches slammed into me and knocked me down as a sizzling blue beam shot through the space where I'd been standing moments before. It hit a Darkanist, disintegrating him before he could form a scream.

I rolled to my feet and formed Ebonsoul.

<Thanks, boy>

<Stay away from the blue energy. It is bad.>

Several of the Darkanists formed blades and approached. Around us, other Darkanists were focused on attacking Monty and Lotus, while still others had their arms extended and were beaming light-blue energy at Gault.

*<Got it. Stop those mages, especially the ones with the blue energy. If they try to hurt you, hurt them first.>*

He growled and blinked out. I heard the screams a few seconds later and smiled. Three Darkanists wielding blades approached slowly. I counted five more behind them, all also holding blades in their hands.

Eight against one. It was almost a fair fight.

"I'm only going to make this offer once," I said, holding Ebonsoul across my body in a defensive stance. "Leave now and you leave with your lives. Fight me and I will make sure I'm the only one walking away."

A few in the back mocked me, and laughed. The three closest to me tightened their grips, and nodded.

"You're not even a mage," one of the Darkanists in front of me scoffed. "We're going to cut you down and make you beg for your life."

"And you are?"

"What does it matter to you?" he asked, as he hefted his blade. "You're dead."

"I'm going to save you for last."

"I'm Henderson, and you're not going to last five seconds, Strong," he said, as they circled me. "That's right. We know who you are, and we know everything about you. You're nothing without the mage, and he's busy trying not to die. Not that he's going to last much longer than you."

More laughter from the back.

"You should have never tried to face the Keeper," another Darkanist said. "You really think you three could stand against him? This was a suicide mission. You're dead—you just don't know it yet."

"Sometimes the stupid is just so flagrant, it hurts to watch," I heard TK comment from behind the five in the back. "Are these supposed to be guards?"

TK?

I tried to look around the three mages in front of me but my vision was blocked and they weren't budging. Having three rune-covered blades pointed at you had a way of narrowing your focus.

"I don't know, love, they don't look like they're guarding much," LD answered. "Show them the error of their ways."

It wasn't the Ten, but it was nearly as good.

"I think it's too late for that," she said, "but we can't have them interfering, now, can we?"

"You know what he said—clear the field and leave the Keeper to these three," LD said. "I guess you can leave those three. I'll take care of the rest of these mages."

"Very well," TK said. "Simon, Tristan needs your assistance. Stop dallying and dispatch these mages."

"You heard her, hombre. Get with it," LD said. "You don't have all day."

TK unleashed a barrage of green orbs into the five mages in the back as LD flung several gray circles at the mages attacking Monty and Lotus. Henderson lunged at me, attempting to bury his blade in my midsection. I parried his thrust and pivoted, dropping the Darkanist to my left with a right cross.

The second Darkanist slashed at me, trying to force me back into Henderson, who was at my rear. Instead of backing up, I stepped forward, jamming the attack with Ebonsoul and driving an elbow into the attacker's face. His nose erupted with a gush of blood as I followed up the first elbow strike with a second. He crumpled to the ground, unconscious.

I saw TK step back and tap her wrist as I glanced at her.

"Remember, *tempus edax rerum.*"

The next second, both TK and LD were gone.

"Your friends have left you," Henderson said, but the fight was gone from his voice. "It's over."

"My friends have places to be and Keepers to stop," I said,

focusing on him. "I told you, I was leaving you for last."

"I'm going to kill you, Strong."

He lunged forward and slashed wide at my face, overextending himself. I moved back and let the attack pass before stepping in, trapping his blade with one hand as I absorbed Ebonsoul.

"What happened?" he mocked, as he struggled against the trap. "I knew you were soft. Lost your blade and your nerve."

"Not exactly," I said, reforming Ebonsoul in my hand and hitting him hard against the temple with the hilt. "You're not worth it."

"Coward," he slurred as he took several steps back. "Mercy...is for the...for the weak."

"Only the truly strong can show mercy," I said as he fell back unconscious. "Goodnight."

I reabsorbed Ebonsoul and ran down to the amphitheater, stopping at the edge. The flow of energy from the center of the amphitheater washed over me and nearly knocked me off my feet.

Peaches had finished off the rest of the Darkanists, and if I focused, I could sense the battle at the footbridge. It would be over soon, now that TK and LD had joined Nightwing.

In the center of the amphitheater, I saw Gault with both arms extended. Thick blue beams flowed from his fingers, aimed at Monty and Lotus. Monty was keeping the blue beam back with a golden-white beam of his own, but I could tell he was struggling.

Lotus was using a blue beam herself, lighter than Gault's, but still strong enough to slow his beam down. She was struggling, too. I could see Gault's beams slowly moving forward.

Both of them were trapped in some kind of energy cage from their waists down, keeping them locked in place. Gault had created large blue circles under their feet, which pulsed with blue flashes every few seconds.

"Welcome, Strong," Gault said, his voice casual, as if we were sitting in a cafe having lunch. "You've come to witness the end of everything and the beginning of a new age."

Peaches rumbled next to my leg.

*<Not yet, boy. Not yet.>*

"I'm here to stop you," I said. "Monty's not going to give you the First Elder Rune. He'd rather die first."

"A sentiment he shared with me. I thought I would oblige his request," Gault said, glancing at Monty. "There's nothing you can do but watch. You lack the power to approach me, much less stop me. Mage Montague has what is rightfully mine, and the Lotus will facilitate the transfer. What can you possibly do but witness as I unleash glorious entropy?"

I glanced over at Monty as he struggled to keep Gault's beam back. We locked eyes for a moment, but everything we needed to say was said in that one glance.

I looked over at Lotus who stared fiercely in my direction. She nodded once and turned to focus on Gault.

*<Can you do it, boy?>*

*<We may not survive if we get closer to the Keeper. Are you sure?>*

*<We have to stop him. If we don't, everything dies.>*

*<Stand close. This will hurt.>*

*<It's only pain.>*

I buried my hand in the scruff of his neck as he howled and then released an ear-shattering bark. Heat blossomed in my stomach as I felt Peaches grow beside me. Bright red runes formed on my forearms as my skin darkened, growing black with a silver tint.

The runes on the flanks on Peaches' body blazed with red and violet energy, matching the runes on my arms. Peaches' body transformed as he grew, becoming muscular and broader.

There was pain, and I embraced it, welcoming it, as it tore

through my body, transforming me. I felt the change in my body as I became heavier and my skin became denser and thicker.

I smiled at the sensation of agony.

It was familiar, like an old friend.

I let it wash over me and fully accepted it as power flowed into my body.

*<Let's go, boy.>*

*<I am right behind you. Where you go, I go.>*

Peaches barked and tore up a trench in the ground in front of us, which ended at Gault. I stepped into the trench as the energy from the Keeper slammed into me. Peaches stood behind me, nudging me forward with his head.

Each step was a battle, and Gault laughed every time I stumbled and fell to one knee. Every time, I would manage to get back up and move forward.

"How quaint," Gault said, with a smile. "You think a mere battle form transformation will allow you to face me? Whatever power you now possess is still no match for my suppression field. It is impenetrable."

"We'll see," I managed through clenched teeth and took another step forward.

"Those remaining ten feet may as well be ten thousand miles," he scoffed. "I am a Keeper; my power dwarfs yours. In moments, my beams will reach the Mage and the Lotus, and I will begin the transfer of the First Elder Rune. What you are trying to do is hopeless. Surrender and accept the end."

*<Boy, can you still bark?>*

*<I can, but if I speak now it will strike you. I am directly behind you.>*

*<I can't reach him on my own, but if you bark——>*

*<The blast of my bark while in this form can kill you.>*

*<We don't have much of a choice, boy. Your bark can help me cross the remaining feet.>*

*<What will you do if you manage to get close to him? I am at my limit.>*

*<I still have one option, but I can't show it yet.>*

*<You would risk it all on a theory?>*

*<If it means I have a chance at saving you, saving my family? Yes.>*

*<And if you die in the process? Really die this time?>*

*<Still worth it. Will you do it?>*

*<Yes...you are my bondmate.>*

*<Give me three more steps. I'll be closer, and then we'll see how impenetrable his field really is.>*

I took another step forward as Kali's words came back to me: *The day is fast approaching when you will have to choose between creation and destruction. Which will you choose, my Marked One?*

I didn't think she meant today, but with Kali you never knew. It didn't matter if today was the day or if it was centuries from now—I had made my choice. Even though I may have been the Marked of Kali, today, I chose creation over destruction.

I took another step forward, but sensed that Peaches had remained where he was. The waves of energy lashed against me, threatening to shove me back. I noticed that my clothes were being rapidly shredded; blue energy tore at the fabric and slowly destroyed it.

When I looked closer, I saw that parts of my skin were going through the same thing. Trails of blue energy were cutting grooves into my skin, slowly disintegrating me.

"You realize the futility of your actions now," Gault said, sounding almost sad. "Now, when you cannot be saved. The field will blast you away once I start the transfer. You could have witnessed the death and birth of the universe before your demise. Now, all you will be is a memory that will fade away with time."

I took another step forward.

I felt Peaches' intake of breath as he inhaled. It almost pulled me back as he took an enormous breath. I sensed him take the three steps to get close as he placed his muzzle against my back, and then he barked.

I formed Ebonsoul as the energy from my hellhound's bark tore through me and pushed me forward. The power and energy from his bark slammed up against the suppression field, causing ripple effects all around me. With both arms, I strained as I held Ebonsoul in front me, pushing through the suppression field. It was slow at first, and Gault looked at me with amusement in his eyes. That soon turned to wariness, and finally fear as I picked up speed.

The runes on Ebonsoul's blade blazed a bright white as I cut through the field and buried Ebonsoul in Gault's throat. He looked at me with shock on his face as he retracted his blue beams. The cages of energy around Lotus and Monty vanished, along with the circles under their feet.

"You dare?" Gault rasped, grabbing me by the neck and squeezing as Ebonsoul disappeared. "You dare!"

"Opening," I managed as Gault squeezed the air out of my throat. "Take it."

Lotus rushed up to Gault and gestured, unleashing her light blue beams. She placed a hand on his chest, and extended her other arm to Monty. Monty gestured and his body suddenly became covered with golden white energy.

The First Elder Rune.

"You wanted this?" Monty said, as he activated the rune. "It's all yours now."

Monty blasted a golden-white beam at Lotus, who received it in her outstretched hand. It traveled through her body and punched into Gault with a deep *thrum*. I was launched away from Gault the moment the energy slammed into him.

Just like before, they were locked together—except this time, it was Monty firing a beam of energy into Lotus, who was transferring it into Gault.

"Fools!" Gault yelled. "This is exactly what I wanted. You're giving me the First Elder Rune. Yes!"

"Not exactly," Lotus said, before whispering a group of words I couldn't understand. "You didn't know I knew the command for your seal, but my sight wasn't limited to just what I could see."

A beam of black energy shot up into the sky from Lotus' shoulder and quickly reversed direction, enveloping Gault and Lotus in a cocoon of darkness.

"You wanted entropy," Lotus said. "Allow it to embrace you."

"No...no! "Gault screamed. "Not like this! I am a Keeper!"

Blue light flared out from the cocoon, attempting to break free, but the darkness was too strong, too absolute. It swallowed the blue light and began to spread out along the ground.

"Monty," I said, looking at the ground. "That doesn't look good. Can you stop it?"

Monty collapsed to his knees next to me.

"I'm going to take that as a no," I said, looking around. "Monty?"

"You will not stop me," Gault yelled, and Lotus flew out of the darkness in a blast of blue light. She landed on the ground next to me with a grunt of pain, and covered in darkness. "You think you can stop me with a cast of my own making?"

Gault, like Lotus, was still covered in darkness, and it was continuing to spread.

I got unsteadily to my feet and formed Ebonsoul as Monty rose to one knee. Peaches gave a weak growl, but I knew he was done—we all were. I kept an eye on the darkness and realized we should have been looking for a way off the island.

But Gault was still alive.

"Bloody hell," Monty said under his breath as he stood. "I really thought that would work."

"Me too," I said, trying to tighten my grip around Ebonsoul. "How many tries do you have left?"

"One," he said. "The first one brought us to a stalemate. You just saw the second."

"Which leaves us—"

"With nothing," Gault said with a dark laugh. "Even now, the containment cast inside the mage is compromised. This will be your burial ground. You may have ended my plan, but I will survive this, and you will not. Shortsighted fools. I have defeated you all. The First Elder Rune will still be mine. I only need to wait for the next Keeper rotation."

"No!" Lotus screamed from behind me as she stripped Ebonsoul from my grip and lunged at Gault. He turned just in time for her to plunge it in his chest. "Die!"

"Stupid child," he said as he grabbed her. "This weapon failed to kill me once. What makes you think it will be successful—"

The white runes along Ebonsoul's blade erupted with white light. The same white light formed inside Lotus, and a tether of golden-white energy formed between them.

The darkness, which had been receding up to this point, shot up and wrapped itself around Gault, flinging Lotus away. Gault began laughing as the darkness began overtaking the golden white energy.

"I control this," Gault said, looking down at his body. "This is my power. With this, I will remake the universe."

"Simon, grab Lotus," Monty said as he began moving back. "Now."

The darkness had begun to spread aggressively now,

devouring the island beneath us. I picked up Lotus and moved fast as Monty ran ahead. Behind us, Gault screamed and laughed as the darkness consumed him.

"Is he dead?" I said, not daring to look back. "Tell me he's dead, Monty. Those screams sound like a dead man."

"Worse—he's being unmade by an entropic dissolution," Monty said when we reached the edge of the darkness. "He's being consumed."

I turned, then, and looked.

Gault was missing parts of his body. There were gaping holes forming all over him. He looked down at the holes and laughed some more.

"This can't stop me!" he yelled. "Nothing can stop me!"

"What happened?" I asked. "I thought the First Elder Rune failed?"

"Time," Monty said, "is the devourer of all things. The entropic dissolution was delayed by Lotus and the First Elder Rune. Once your blade activated the siphon, it interrupted the transfer. I still have the First Elder Rune...I need to take a brisk swim in the Thames."

"You what?" I said, turning to see Monty fall back on the ground. He was burning up. "What's wrong?"

"Cast...containment cast failing," he said. "It's too late..needed to transfer First Elder Rune before...before collapse." He closed his eyes and took a deep breath. "This is...this is utter rubbish."

"Is there anything I can do?"

"I don't suppose you could make a good cuppa?" he said as sweat poured down his face. "No, Simon, there's nothing you can do, but we won. We stopped him."

"This is not a win!" I said. "Use that huge mage brain of yours. There has to be something we can do. Think!"

"There is something we can do, but I don't know how to do it," Lotus said, still covered in darkness. "I don't have much time, and neither does Tristan. I can't be saved, but he can be—if Evergreen were here. Do you know how to open portals?"

"I don't, but I know someone who does."

*<Boy! Bring the Green Keeper here now! I don't care where you have to go to find him. Bring him here or Monty dies. Find him and bring him here, now!>*

Peaches blinked out and each second felt like a lifetime.

I counted three seconds before my amazing hellhound returned with his massive jaws wrapped around Evergreen's arm.

Evergreen took one look at the situation and raced over to where Monty lay. He then pulled Lotus close and shook his head at her.

"It's too late for you, my child, but we can save the mage," Evergreen said. "Are you willing to do this? Will you sacrifice your life so that he can live?"

"If that is the cost that must be paid, I pay it gladly," she said with a smile. "Gault has been destroyed. My purpose is fulfilled. Do what you must."

Evergreen gestured and formed a large, golden circle beneath the three of them as he sat on the ground. He placed a hand on Monty's brow and held Lotus' hand as he said some words of power. The circle shifted around them, turning counterclockwise before turning clockwise. It kept rotating, picking up speed until it was only a blur of symbols and energy underneath them.

A golden-white light rose from Monty and formed a sphere. It floated over to Lotus who extended her hand. The light rested on her hand for a moment before traveling up her arm and into her chest. It slowly reformed in the hand that was clasped with Evergreen's.

Evergreen's energy signature expanded with power as he reclaimed his primal rune. As he opened his eyes, gleaming golden energy flowed from them. He scanned Monty for a few seconds and hovered a hand over his body. More wisps of energy—some red, some black, and some violet—flowed into Evergreen's hand. When he was satisfied, he looked over at Lotus.

"I could try to reverse—" he started.

"No," Lotus said. "This is how it should be. I only ever wanted one thing, and now I have that."

"Is there anything else you would like?" Evergreen said, sadness filling his voice. "Anything?"

"Yes," Lotus said, looking down at her body. "Could you finish this dissolution? I don't want to die like he did. Can you make it fast?"

"I can," Evergreen said, getting to his feet. He bowed deeply to her. "Thank you, Lotus."

She returned the bow and closed her eyes.

Evergreen gestured and a sphere of golden energy formed around Lotus. With another gesture, the sphere floated up and disappeared into the sky.

Lotus was gone.

A huge rumbling and cracking sound shot through the island at that moment. I looked down and saw that, at the edge of the darkness that had undone Gault, the island was gone.

"That can't be good," I said, pointing at the ground. "There's nothing there."

"I fear this entire island has been compromised," Evergreen said, forming a large golden circle under us. "We best be off." He looked up into the distance and then nodded. "Everyone is secure and off the island. It's time to go."

With another gesture, golden light filled my vision, and we left what remained of the Little Island.

# TWENTY-THREE

I sat in Evergreen's cabin enjoying a steaming mug of Death-wish coffee. Looking out of one of the windows, I gazed over a barren landscape which was, in its own way, beautiful.

My hellhound snored at my feet after devouring three bowls of pastrami that should have shattered his stomach. I glanced down at him and shook my head; I was seriously going to have to put him on a diet.

Evergreen sat across from me and gazed out of the window.

"I was fully prepared for a second War of the Keepers," he said, quietly as he sipped from his cup. "You and Tristan..." He glanced over at the futon where Monty was lying. "You truly surprised me."

"You took back the entire elder rune?"

"Yes," he said. "I have it in its entirety."

"What else did you take, there at the end?" I asked, focusing on him. "You took more than the elder rune."

"I took all the runes, major and minor," he said. "I had to."

"Why?"

"They were obstructing his shift to Archmage," he said, after taking another sip from his cup. He was drinking more of the honey-gold liquid Monty had given me when I was injured. "Without the elder runes, I was able to align his path. His shift will be soon."

"You made him stronger?"

"No. I only removed the obstacles to his natural shift," he said. "He should have been an Archmage by now. He is naturally gifted. Acquiring the runes caused a deviation in his path. It allowed darkness to taint his ability."

"You removed his darkness?"

"No one can remove darkness, Simon," he said, looking out of the window again. "I removed the runes he was not yet ready to know."

"What if he finds them again?"

"He may," Evergreen admitted. "The Montagues have always been ahead of their peers when it comes to their abilities. It's quite possible he may seek them out again. I did leave the palms he learned—those will prove useful."

"But not the blood runes?"

"Blood magic of any kind is dangerous. He's not ready to learn or use it yet," Evergreen answered. "Perhaps in a few centuries, when he's matured some."

I took another sip of my amazing javambrosia and enjoyed the silence.

"How long can we stay here?" I asked. "I mean, really, how long?"

Evergreen smiled as if reading my mind.

"You can stay here as long as you need," he said. "Time does not flow the same here. Is that what you wanted to hear?"

"Yes, but that's not the truth, is it?"

"Which part?"

"The part about staying here as long as we need," I said. "I need at least fifty years of a break."

Evergreen laughed and his eyes gleamed with golden light.

"You cannot take a fifty-year break, I'm sorry to say," he said. "Would you really want that long of a break?"

I gave the question some thought.

"No, not if I'm being honest," I said. "We prevented the entropic dissolution of our plane. No one even knows what we did."

"There are some who know."

"Really? And we'll probably still get blamed for sinking Little Island."

"There are two groups of people who will know of your deeds," Evergreen said. "And you need to be wary of both."

"Which two?"

"Those who will heap praise on you, but try to take you from the path of who and what you are. With those, let the praise fall on deaf ears."

"And the other group?"

"Those who will plot to undo you, by destroying who and what you love the most," he said. "With those, make your ears sharper than your hellhound's."

"How will I know the difference between the two groups?"

"Have you considered that the odds of your survival up to this point have been astronomically small?"

"It has crossed my mind once or twice."

"How have you survived this long?" he asked, a smile around his eyes. "Have you given this thought?"

"More than once, yes," I answered, thinking he may have been trying to insult me, but I saw nothing but genuine concern in his eyes. "I have Monty, Peaches, and everyone else. I have my family. That's the only way I've made it this far."

"That is how you will be able to determine the difference between the groups."

I smiled, knowing he was right. I took another long pull from my mug and enjoyed the silence a bit more.

"Use this time to hone your abilities," he continued. "You need to get control of your battle form, and Tristan will have to go through a process of re-education."

"He's going to be extra-grumpy about that," I said, and smiled at the thought of Monty having to relearn casts. "We may need to extend the stay just a bit."

Evergreen laughed.

"It's not going to be smooth sailing for you or your hellhound, either," he said. "From my understanding, learning the lowest phase of the battle form is arduous and difficult work."

I groaned.

"Can we start that tomorrow?"

Evergreen nodded.

"Take today and rest," he said. "Tomorrow, we will begin your training."

He stood and left the room, leaving me alone with the view, my coffee, and the knowledge that my life had just gotten much, much harder.

THE END

# AUTHOR NOTES

**Thank you for reading this story and jumping into the world of Monty & Strong with me.**

*Disclaimer: The Author Notes are written at the very end of the writing process. This section is not seen by the ART or my amazing Jeditor—Audrey. Any typos or errors following this disclaimer are mine and mine alone.*

I'm with Kali on this one.

*You have matured. Not much, but you have certainly grown since we last spoke.*

I find that as the stories progress, Simon is acquiring a certain gravitas. He's not quite on Monty's level (I don't think that will ever happen), but his default answer to most situations he's facing isn't always a smartass answer. This is not to say that he isn't a smartass lol, he wouldn't be Simon if he didn't have some snark in his personality, but as Kali said, he is growing.

Is this a good thing?

I think so.

He can only be in awe of the new world he moves in for so

long. At some point he has to understand that abnormal is his new normal. The shift in his sarcastic way of being is also because he's losing the mind-numbing fear (he's down to blood-chilling fear these days, I think) and with that loss of fear, his coping strategy has to evolve as well.

This story (book 21? WOW! Hard to believe this is book 21!) is almost a reset and deepening of the stakes for the Terrible Trio. The powers that are behind the scenes are now noticing them, and this is not a good thing. Unlocking the battle form with Peaches, has just painted a huge target on Simon's back (and front), and Monty having to relearn casts means he's been knocked down a few rungs on the mage ladder, but with the potential to reach Archmage sooner.

It also means they are vulnerable as they enter their glass cannon phase. They are incredibly dangerous and incredibly delicate as they grow in power. It's a strange paradox, but that's how it makes sense in my head. Let's roll with it.

The next book, CORPSE ROAD reintroduces Estilete as a Blood Heretic with a grudge (losing an arm tends to make you angry and plan torturous schemes of vengeance) along with a new ability that awakens in Simon due to Ebonsoul being a necrotic blade...*he sees dead people*. Won't spoil it more than that :).

They will have to deal with the Sanguinary Order, pay a visit to Hades, the place and the god, and make a detour to the sacred city of Caral in Peru. There is a key to the central issue of the story hidden in that city and it needs to be found and used.

In the next few books, Simon's life is going to go from bad to horrific, Dira will step up her game (she wants to be the Marked One), Shadow Hounds will be after him and Peaches, a certain group of necromancers won't appreciate the fact that he can now interact with the dead (that's their department after all) and will look to retire him permanently. Yes, the irony is thick there.

In addition, there needs to be that conversation with Badb Catha (scary!) and what it means to work with her and when that will start. Oh, I nearly forgot, Kali would like to have a few more words with her Marked One. There seem to be some unresolved issues about his thwarting her plan against Shiva.

On Monty's side, losing the elder runes will cause an inner conflict. Some of his casts will fail because the foundation of his will has been shaken. He needs to confront why he stepped into a gray area and reconcile his new life without the blood casts.

He also faces a choice.

Relearn the blood magic or continue without it. Several powerful mages, dark and light, are watching him and waiting to see what he decides.

This book closes the trilogy mini arc (LOST RUNES, ARCHMAGE, ENTROPY) within the larger series. Seriously, as I write this, it's hard to wrap my head around this series being at 21 books and counting.

This is the part where I cut and paste from my previous notes because it's so important:

*I want to sincerely thank you for joining me in this adventure, these are by far the easiest and hardest stories for me to tell, but your being there with me for each part of this adventure makes it worthwhile.*

*Read that last paragraph again, go ahead, I'll wait.*

*I may write the stories, but, as I said in a recent episode of the MoB Kaffeeklatsch, there is one character that is in every story I write—you. Every story I write is like sharing an adventure with you and I'm here for it...for all of it.*

*You, as the reader, are important to me and my storytelling, and I hope we can share so many more stories in the future, until we are sharing them with the next generation and the generations after them.*

Cut and paste done.

I do sincerely mean every word. You are essential to my storytelling and I am privileged and honored to be able to share these amazing adventures with you.

You are amazing.

What else is happening? I'm so glad you asked.

Treadwell book two—SHADOW QUEEN is being worked on and promises to be fun, dark, and dare I say it, have some elements of romance? (Say it isn't so!) Not romance in the usual sense, this is me after all. I may have to create a new sub-genre of romance (Urban Fantasy Nomance?) for authors who don't really want to write it, but have to lol.

I do truly cringe when I write it, but I'm getting better. Don't expect the usual romance, this is going to be romance very much in the vein of Alice and Luther (IYKYK) and it will be unexpected, dark, and dangerous.

Sebastian and Regina have a complicated relationship. One that will make Sebastian's life incredibly difficult and quite possibly shove him into some lethal situations he would prefer to avoid. That should be fun.

CORPSE ROAD (M&S 22) is also in early stages. I have to do a bunch of research if we are going to Peru, in addition to dealing with Death Cults and necromancy. Turns out Orethe had friends, and those friends would like a word with Simon.

It promises to be an twisted and fun story. Some old characters from the earlier stories will be making cameo appearances and some new characters will be introduced.

I know that most of the time these notes sound super cryptic, and for that I apologize. I'm excited to reveal as much as possible, but I'm also aware that revealing too much, too early would spoil the stories for you. That, I don't want to do.

At this point we've been together for six years (T&B was published in Feb of 2017) and many of you have been here since the Spiritual Warriors (Aug 2012), which means you've been on this crazy ride with me for eleven years.

I can only say THANK YOU (and WOW!).

I am humbled and deeply honored that you would join me in the creations of my semi-twisted imagination as we drive, fly, and explode our way through the worlds of my mind.

I think I can safely say that after all this time, we are just hitting our stride, which means, load up the extra large thermos with Death Wish (extra-extra), slide into the Dark Goat (shove the creature vaguely resembling a canine to one side, if he lets you. Sausage might help.), strap in tight and hold on.

We have plans to foil, evil to thwart, people to save, casts to learn, and property to destroy!

As always, remembering the sage words of our resident Zen Hellhound Master...

Meat is Life!

**Thank you again for jumping into this story with me!**

## BITTEN PEACHES PUBLISHING

### Thanks for Reading!

If you enjoyed this book, would you please **leave a review** at the site you purchased it from? It doesn't have to be long... just a line or two would be fantastic and it would really help me out.

### Bitten Peaches Publishing offers more books and audiobooks

across various genres including: urban fantasy, science fiction, adventure, & mystery!

www.BittenPeachesPublishing.com

### More books by Orlando A. Sanchez

### Montague & Strong Detective Agency Novels

Tombyards & Butterflies•Full Moon Howl•Blood is Thicker•Silver Clouds Dirty Sky•Homecoming•Dragons & Demigods•Bullets & Blades•Hell Hath No Fury•Reaping Wind•The Golem•Dark Glass•Walking the

Razor•Requiem•Divine Intervention•Storm
Blood•Revenant•Blood Lessons•Broken Magic•Lost
Runes•Archmage•Entropy

## Montague & Strong Detective Agency Stories
No God is Safe•The Date•The War Mage•A Proper
Hellhound•The Perfect Cup•Saving Mr. K

## Night Warden Novels
Wander•ShadowStrut•Nocturne Melody

## Rule of the Council
Blood Ascension•Blood Betrayal•Blood Rule

## The Warriors of the Way
The Karashihan•The Spiritual Warriors•The Ascendants•The
Fallen Warrior•The Warrior Ascendant•The Master Warrior

## John Kane
The Deepest Cut•Blur

## Sepia Blue
The Last Dance•Rise of the
Night•Sisters•Nightmare•Nameless•Demon

## Chronicles of the Modern Mystics
The Dark Flame•A Dream of Ashes

## The Treadwell Supernatural Directive
The Stray Dogs

## Brew & Chew Adventures
Hellhound Blues

## Bangers & Mash
Bangers & Mash

## Tales of the Gatekeepers
Bullet Ballet•The Way of Bug•Blood Bond

## Division 13
The Operative•The Magekiller

## Blackjack Chronicles
The Dread Warlock

## The Assassin's Apprentice
The Birth of Death

## Gideon Shepherd Thrillers
Sheepdog

## DAMNED
Aftermath

## Nyxia White
They Bite•They Rend•They Kill

## Iker the Cleaner
Iker the Unseen•Daystrider•Nightwalker

Stay up to date with new releases!
Shop www.orlandoasanchez.com for more books and
audiobooks!

## CONTACT ME

To send me a message, email me at:
orlando@orlandoasanchez.com

### Join our newsletter:
www.orlandoasanchez.com

Stay up to date with new releases and audiobooks!
**Shop:** www.orlandoasanchez.com

For more information on the M&S World...come join the
MoB Family on Facebook!
You can find us at:
Montague & Strong Case Files

Visit our online M&S World Swag Store located at:
Emandes

For exclusive stories...join our Patreon!
Patreon

Please follow our amazing instagram page at:
bittenpeaches

Follow us on Youtube:
Bitten Peaches Publishing Storyteller

If you enjoyed the book, **please leave a review**. Reviews help the book, and also help other readers find good stories to read.

**THANK YOU!**

## ART SHREDDERS

I want to take a moment to extend a special thanks to the ART SHREDDERS.

No book is the work of one person. I am fortunate enough to have an amazing team of advance readers and shredders.

Thank you for giving of your time and keen eyes to provide notes, insights, answers to the questions, and corrections (dealing wonderfully with my extreme dreaded comma allergy). You help make every book and story go from good to great. Each and every one of you helped make this book fantastic, and I couldn't do this without each of you.

### THANK YOU

### <u>ART SHREDDERS</u>

Amber, Anne Morando, Audrey Cienki,
Cat, Chris Christman II
Daniel Parr, Dawn, Denise King, Diane Craig, Dolly Sanchez, Donna Young Hatridge

Hal Bass, Helen

Jasmine Breeden, Jasmine Davis, Jeanette Auer, Jen Cooper, Joy Kiili, Jules AD, Julie Peckett

Karen Hollyhead

Larry Diaz Tushman, Laura Tallman I, Luann Zipp

Marcia Campbell, Mari de Valerio, Maryelaine Eckerle-Foster, Melissa Miller, Melody DeLoach, Michelle Blue

Paige Guido

RC Battels, Rene Corrie, Rob Farnham, Rohan Gandhy

Sara Madon Branson, Sondra Massey, Stacey Stein, Susie Johnson

Tami Cowles, Ted Camer, Terri Adkisson, Tommy Owens

Vikki Brannagan

Wendy Schindler

# PATREON SUPPORTERS

## TO ALL OUR PATRONS

I want to extend a special note of gratitude to all of our
Patrons in
**The Magick Squad.**

Your generous support helps me to continue on this amazing
adventure called "being an author".
I deeply and truly appreciate each of you for your selfless act
of patronage.

You are all amazing beyond belief.
***

If you are not a patron, and would like to enjoy the exclusive
stories available only to our members...join the Squad!

The Magick Squad

## THANK YOU

Alisha Harper, Amber Dawn Sessler, Angela Tapping, Anne Morando, Anthony Hudson, Ashley Britt

Brenda French

Carl Skoll, Carrie O'Leary, Cat Inglis, Chad Bowden, Chris Christman II, Cindy Deporter, Connie Cleary

Dan Fong, Davis Johnson, Diane Garcia, Diane Kassmann, Dorothy Phillips

Elizabeth Barbs, Enid Rodriguez, Eric Maldonato, Eve Bartlet, Ewan Mollison

Federica De Dominicis, Francis August Valanzola

Gail Ketcham Hermann, Gary McVicar, Geoff Siegel, Grace Gemeinhardt, Groove72

Heidi Wolfe

Ingrid Schijven

Jacob Anderson, Jannine Zerres, Jasmine Breeden, Jeffrey Juchau, Jim Maguire, Jo Dungey, Joe Durham, John Fauver, Joy Kiili, Joy T, Just Jeanette

Kathy Ringo, Kimberly Curington, Krista Fox

Lisa Simpson

Malcolm Robertson, Mark Morgan, Mary Barzee, Mary Beth Wright, Marydot Pinto, Maureen McCallan, Mel Brown, Melissa Miller, Meri, Duncanson

Paige Guido, Patricia Pearson, Patrick Gregg

Ralph Kroll, Renee Penn, Robert Walters

Sammy Dawkins, Sara M Branson, Sara N Morgan, Sarah Sofianos, Sassy Bear, Sonyia Roy, Stacey Stein, Susan Spry

Tami Cowles, Terri Adkisson, Tommy

Van Nebedum

Wanda Corder-Jones, Wendy Schindler

# ACKNOWLEDGEMENTS

With each book, I realize that every time I learn something about this craft, it highlights so many things I still have to learn. Each book, each creative expression, has a large group of people behind it.

This book is no different.

Even though you see one name on the cover, it is with the knowledge that I am standing on the shoulders of the literary giants that informed my youth, and am supported by my generous readers who give of their time to jump into the adventures of my overactive imagination.

I would like to take a moment to express my most sincere thanks:

**To Dolly:** My wife and greatest support. You make all this possible each and every day. You keep me grounded when I get lost in the forest of ideas. Thank you for asking the right questions when needed, and listening intently when I go off on tangents. Thank you for who you are and the space you create—I love you.

**To my Tribe:** You are the reason I have stories to tell. You cannot possibly fathom how much and how deeply I love you all.

**To Lee:** Because you were the first audience I ever had. I love you, sis.

**To the Logsdon Family:** The words *thank you* are insufficient to describe the gratitude in my heart for each of you. JL, your support always demands I bring my best, my A-game, and produce the best story I can. Both you and Lorelei (my Uber Jeditor) and now, Audrey, are the reason I am where I am today. My thank you for the notes, challenges, corrections, advice, and laughter. Your patience is truly infinite. *Arigatougozaimasu.*

**To The Montague & Strong Case Files Group—AKA The MoB (Mages of Badassery):** When I wrote T&B there were fifty-five members in The MoB. As of this release, there are over one thousand five hundred members in the MoB. I am honored to be able to call you my MoB Family. Thank you for being part of this group and M&S.

You make this possible. **THANK YOU.**

**To the ever-vigilant PACK:** You help make the MoB...the MoB. Keeping it a safe place for us to share and just...be. Thank you for your selfless vigilance. You truly are the Sentries of Sanity.

**Chris Christman II:** A real-life technomancer who makes the **MoBTV LIVEvents +Kaffeeklatsch** on YouTube amazing. Thank you for your tireless work and wisdom. Everything is connected...you totally rock!

**To the WTA—The Incorrigibles:** JL, Ben Z., Eric QK., S.S., and Noah.

They sound like a bunch of badass misfits, because they are. My exposure to the deranged and deviant brain trust you all represent helped me be the author I am today. I have officially gone to the *dark side* thanks to all of you. I humbly give you my thanks, and...it's all your fault.

**To my fellow Indie Authors:** I want to thank each of you for creating a space where authors can feel listened to, and encouraged to continue on this path. A rising tide lifts all the ships indeed.

**To The English Advisory:** Aaron, Penny, Carrie, Davina, and all of the UK MoB. For all things English...thank you.

**To DEATH WISH COFFEE:** This book (and every book I write) has been fueled by generous amounts of the only coffee on the planet (and in space) strong enough to power my very twisted imagination. Is there any other coffee that can compare? I think not. DEATH WISH—thank you!

**To Deranged Doctor Design:** Kim, Darja, Tanja, Jovana, and Milo (Designer Extraordinaire).

If you've seen the covers of my books and been amazed, you can thank the very talented and gifted creative team at DDD. They take the rough ideas I give them, and produce incredible covers that continue to surprise and amaze me. Each time, I find myself striving to write a story worthy of the covers they produce. DDD, you embody professionalism and creativity. Thank you for the great service and spectacular covers. **YOU GUYS RULE!**

**To you, the reader:** I was always taught to save the best for last. I write these stories for **you**. Thank you for jumping down the rabbit holes of ***what if?*** with me. You are the reason I write the stories I do.

You keep reading...I'll keep writing.

Thank you for your support and encouragement.

## SPECIAL MENTIONS

**To Dolly:** My rock, anchor, and inspiration. Thank you...always.

**Larry & Tammy—The WOUF:** Because even when you aren't there...you're there.

### *Orlando A. Sanchez*
www.orlandoasanchez.com

Orlando has been writing ever since his teens when he was immersed in creating scenarios for playing Dungeons & Dragons with his friends every weekend.

The worlds of his books are urban settings with a twist of the paranormal lurking just behind the scenes and with generous doses of magic, martial arts, and mayhem.

He currently resides in Queens, NY with his wife and children.

## Thanks for Reading!

If you enjoyed this book, would you **please leave a review** at the site you purchased it from? It doesn't have to be a book report... just a line or two would be fantastic and it would really help us out!

Printed in Great Britain
by Amazon